Praise for
the Bluford Series:

"Once I started reading, I couldn't sleep. My hands were sweating and my heart was pumping. I thought something was wrong with me. These books are *that* exciting."
— *Kareem S.*

"I love the Bluford Series because I can relate to the stories and the characters. They are just like real life. Ever since I read the first one, I've been hooked."
— *Jolene P.*

"On a scale of 1–10, the scale breaks if I rate the Bluford Series. They are *that* good!"
— *Cornell C.*

"The last thing I wanted to do was read a Bluford book or any book. But after a few pages, I couldn't put the book down. I felt like I was a witness in the story, like I was inside it."
— *Ray F.*

"I found it very easy to lose myself in these books. They kept my interest from beginning to end and were always realistic. The characters are vivid, and the endings left me in eager anticipation of the next book."
— *Keziah J.*

"Man! These books are amazing!"
— *Dominique J.*

Usually I don't like to read, but I couldn't put the Bluford books down. They kept me interested from beginning to end."

—*Jesus B.*

"My school is just like Bluford High. The characters are just like people I know. These books are real!"

—*Jessica K.*

"I thought the Bluford Series was going to be boring, but once I started, I couldn't stop reading. I had to keep going just to see what would happen next. I have to admit I enjoyed myself. Now I'm done, and I can't wait for more books."

—*Jamal C.*

"All the Bluford books are great. There wasn't one that I didn't like, and I read them all— twice!"

—*Sequoyah D.*

"I've been reading these books for the last three days and can't get them out of my mind. They are *that* good!"

—*Stephen B.*

"Each Bluford book gives you a story that could happen to anyone. The details make you feel like you are inside the books. The storylines are amazing and realistic. I loved them all."

—*Elpiclio B.*

"All my friends and I agree. The Bluford Series is bangin'."

—*Margarita R.*

Search for Safety

John Langan

Series Editor: Paul Langan

TOWNSEND PRESS
www.townsendpress.com

YA
LANG

Books in the Bluford Series

Copyright © 2007 by Townsend Press, Inc.
Printed in the United States of America

9 8 7 6 5

Cover illustration © 2007 by Gerald Purnell

ISBN-13: 978-1-59194-070-8
ISBN-10: 1-59194-070-2

Library of Congress Control Number:
2006924490

Chapter 1

"Larry and I are getting married," my mom announced.

We were at the small kitchen table in my Aunt Fay's apartment. My aunt was across from me grading her students' homework. She's an eighth grade teacher who also taught summer school. I was eating pancakes and almost choked when I heard the news.

"*What?!*" Aunt Fay asked, dropping her pen. "You've only been seeing him for a few months. If things are still good after a year or so, *then* marry him. Right now seems too soon, Geneva. You're not pregnant, so why are you rushing?"

Aunt Fay was right. It was too fast.

Larry Taylor and Mom started seeing each other May of my freshman year at Lincoln High School. Now it was only

August. During the whole time, Larry hardly said a word to me when he came to pick up my mother. A few times, he gave me a quick handshake, but only when Aunt Fay was watching.

"I'm *not* rushing," Mom replied. "Larry thinks it's the right time, and I think it'll be good for me and Ben to be on our own instead of depending on you for everything. Besides, Larry's already found us a place. We're moving in two weeks."

Two weeks. I couldn't believe it. I didn't want to go anywhere. I liked living with Aunt Fay, reading her books and eating stacks of buttery pancakes after church on Sundays with the sun shining right into her living room. It was better than any place Mom and I ever lived in, but I couldn't say that. I couldn't even speak, I was so upset.

Aunt Fay wasn't happy either. She kept shaking her head like she did whenever something bad happened in our neighborhood. I knew why.

Our neighbor Jackie knew Larry from high school. I'd overheard her telling Aunt Fay about him one night back in July. She said people used to call Larry "The Big Hurt" for all the fights he'd gotten into at school.

"*I wouldn't be surprised if he did time somewhere, the things he and his friends used to do,*" Jackie admitted after seeing him pick up my mom one night. "*But that was fifteen long years ago, Fay. People change,*" she had said. Aunt Fay just grunted. They didn't know I was listening.

No matter what anyone said, Mom saw no problems with Larry. She ignored Aunt Fay's advice. Two weeks later, she made me dress up with a shirt and tie like we were going to church. Instead, we went down to the municipal building and got in a line with a bunch of other people. Then an old judge called us into a stuffy conference room, and my mom and Larry were married.

Just like that, I had a stepfather. He didn't look at me the whole time.

The day after the wedding, Mom and I packed our stuff into cardboard boxes and plastic trash bags. Larry came over around noon with a stocky, dark-eyed guy named Donald. Within minutes, they crammed all our things into the back of an old pickup they'd borrowed from somewhere. They left without even saying goodbye to Aunt Fay.

Mom and I followed behind them in Larry's car, and we drove to a rundown row house on Union Street, all the way on the other side of the city. On the way, she dropped another bomb on me.

"You're gonna have to switch to a new school, Ben. It's called Bluford High. Don't worry. Aunt Fay says it's a good school, and Larry says it's no big deal."

What does Larry know? I wanted to say, but I kept my mouth shut as he and Donald quickly unloaded our stuff. They barely talked except when Larry told him what to do or where to put things.

"You get the top floor," Larry grunted to me as I walked into the house for the first time.

He and Donald carried my mattress and old bureau up a narrow stairway that led to the third floor. I followed them, lugging up an old folding chair and a card table.

We entered a small room with a cracked window that faced out onto busy Union Street. The walls were a faded blue, streaked in some places with brown water stains from leaks in the ceiling. A larger back room was empty except for a rusty attic fan mounted in the window. It made a clicking noise when I turned it on and worked only at slow speed.

I spent the rest of the day unpacking and trying to make the dreary room feel like home, but I kept hoping that Mom would change her mind and move back in with Aunt Fay.

It didn't happen.

The next day, I learned Larry's house rules.

It was mid-afternoon, and I was on the couch watching TV when I heard someone unlock the front door. Mom was working her usual shift at the day-care center and wouldn't be back for hours. I figured Larry, a plumber's assistant, had the same schedule. But when he came through the door, I real-ized I was wrong.

"How's it going?" I mumbled to him. It was our first time alone in the house.

"About time we had a chance to talk," he replied, shouldering past me to the kitchen. He came back a second later with a cold beer and grabbed the TV remote that I'd left on the couch.

"There are gonna be days when your mom and I get back from work and wanna just hang out by ourselves. Maybe Donald and some of our friends will come over too, and we'll need space of our own. We're not gonna want a kid around." he paused to drink some beer. "Now you got a nice room upstairs where you can hang out, and I expect you to use it. You with me, *Benny*?"

Making me leave Aunt Fay and move into the beat-up house was bad, but now Larry was trying to boss me around too. I couldn't keep my mouth shut.

"My mom's paying half the rent here, so this is *my* place too," I blurted out. "And my name's *Ben*, not Benny," I added.

Larry snapped. He slammed down his beer and leaped out of his chair, grabbing me by the shirt. I'm five-eight and weigh 140, but Larry was at least six inches taller than me. His arms were solid like the black metal pipes in Aunt Fay's basement. He held my collar so tight, I almost couldn't breathe. For a second, I was helpless.

Get your hands off me! I wanted to say. But I couldn't speak.

"Don't you *ever* talk back to me, Bennyboy," he growled. "And if you don't get upstairs and outta my sight right now, you're gonna wish you never met me."

He shoved me against the wall, and I scrambled away from him. Without a word, I raced up the stairs to my room and tried to lock my door to keep him out. But the old door barely fit in its frame, and I had to ram it shut. It seemed crazy to lock myself in the room, but what else could I do? I didn't want Larry anywhere near me.

About an hour later, I heard the front door slam. I looked out my window and saw Larry get in his old Dodge and drive off. It was past lunchtime, and I was hungry. I figured he'd gone back to work and would be out for hours, so I went downstairs to get something to eat.

Aunt Fay had bought us groceries to take with us when we moved, so the kitchen was already stocked with food. First I had a big bowl of corn flakes, and then I made a cheese sandwich. I was pouring myself a glass of orange juice when I heard a car door slam outside. I looked at the clock. It was way too early for Mom to get home.

My stomach sank.

I put my glass down on the counter and darted toward the stairs. I was halfway there when the front door opened. It was Larry. He was carrying a Budweiser twelve-pack. I wanted to get up the steps before he came in, but I wasn't fast enough.

"*What are you doing here?!*"

Larry's voice boomed through the living room, and his face twisted in anger.

"I just wanted to get something to eat," I said, trying to calm him down. "I'm going back to my room right now." I moved toward the stairs, but Larry stepped in front of me, putting the twelve-pack down.

"When I want you upstairs, you *stay* upstairs!" he yelled.

"But I—"

Whap! Larry cuffed me hard in the jaw with the back of his hand, snapping my head back and splitting my lip. I could taste the blood in my mouth as I stumbled away from him, stunned.

Just get to the stairs, I told myself. I could hear him following me.

I got to the first step when Larry kicked me with his heavy black work boot. The impact slammed against the back of my leg, and I spilled forward on my face, smashing my arms against the hard wooden stairs.

"What are you doing?!" I yelled.

"You're gonna learn to listen to me, one way or the other," he growled, kicking me again in my hip and my backside. I scrambled upward as if my life depended on it. I couldn't believe I was in this nightmare.

Larry kept coming. I reached the second floor landing, sprinted down the short hallway, and raced up the third-floor steps. But I could hear Larry's heavy footsteps behind me. I managed to shut and lock the door to my room, but Larry was there pounding on it just seconds later.

"Open up, or I'll knock it down!" he yelled. I heard him crash his full weight into the door. The rotting frame began to split and crack. I had no choice but to open it up. Larry stood there, his eyes blazing like a madman's, his heavy fists opening and closing.

I had nowhere to run and no idea what to do. I backed away from him but tripped over my mattress and fell. He stepped forward, his heavy boots just inches from my face. If he kicked me now, he'd break my ribs or worse. I never felt so helpless. I winced, bracing myself for the next impact. But instead of hitting me again, Larry stood over me glaring down.

"I want *respect*, Bennyboy. Don't you *ever* come down after I tell you to get upstairs. You hear me?" He nudged my shoulder with the thick square toe of his boot.

"I hear you," I said, my voice just above a whisper. He went on about how it was his house but he was cutting me a break this first time. Then he strode out of my room.

When Mom returned home later that afternoon, I could hear her and Larry arguing. Then I heard her climb the stairs to their second-floor bedroom. I knew she was changing out of her work clothes. It's what she always did after she got home. A few minutes later, I heard her flip-flops slapping against the wooden stairs that led to my room. I stayed on the mattress as she walked in and sat down on the folding chair.

"Ben, don't be giving Larry a hard time," she said. "When he gets home from work, he needs time to himself. Just do what he says and stay out of his way."

I looked quickly at my mom and then turned away, my lip still swollen from where he'd backhanded me.

I knew Mom was tired. The weariness in her voice told me she'd had another long day at the daycare center. Maybe someone called out sick, or the kids were acting up again, or a parent got upset about something. I'd heard all the stories she'd told Aunt Fay. And with our move to Union Street, things were harder. Mom's bus ride now was almost an hour long, but I didn't care. None of that made what Larry did right.

"It'll be okay, Ben. Just give him some time," she said. "He's not used to having a kid in the house. I know he'll come around. You'll see."

"But this is our house too," I said, not even looking at her. My eyes started to burn.

"He and I are paying the rent, not you, Ben. You've got to make the best of our situation. We want to make this work."

My heart sank at her words. Mom wasn't going to stand up for me. She'd married Larry, and if push came to shove she was going to take *his* side, not mine.

I closed my eyes and forced the tears back. My mother put her hand on my shoulder, but I shrugged it away. She

Chapter 2

The next morning, I went down to the kitchen as soon as Larry and Mom left for work. I knew it was the best time to avoid Larry, but as I finished my cereal, I heard someone at the front door. For a second, I thought he was back, and my heart started pounding. But when I peeked out the window, I saw Aunt Fay smiling back at me.

At least she was still on my side.

"Good morning, Ben!" she said, hugging me as soon as I opened the door. She was wearing a blue business suit and looked important, like the women on the TV news.

"I have a surprise for you," she announced, pausing to examine my face. "What happened to you? That bruise looks painful."

"It's nothing," I said almost without thinking. "I banged into a door frame when we were moving in." I was glad my jeans hid my legs.

"Well, at least the move is over," Aunt Fay said. "If you're done breakfast, I want you to come with me. We're going to visit your new school. I have an old friend there I'd like you to meet."

My legs were still sore, and I didn't feel like meeting anyone, but I wasn't about to tell Aunt Fay that. Instead, I ran upstairs, changed into some fresh jeans and a clean T-shirt, and jumped into my aunt's gold Ford Focus.

Aunt Fay drove for about five minutes before we turned into a parking lot next to a giant brick and cinderblock school building. Bluford High School. I'd gone past it a few times but never seen it this close. It was as big as Lincoln, but it also had a full-size outside track and its own football field surrounded by metal bleachers. There was even a sign next to the field.

Welcome to Bluford High School. Home of the Buccaneers, it read.

I started getting nervous, thinking about my first day, when Aunt Fay spoke up.

"The person I want you to meet is Florence Spencer. She's the principal here, and she knows what she's doing. That's one good thing about your move," my aunt said as we got out of her car.

"How do you know her?" I asked.

"We used to work at the same school. Ms. Spencer would teach all day and take graduate classes at night. She became Bluford's principal three years ago," Aunt Fay explained. "I thought you should meet each other before . . . the start of the school year."

For a second Aunt Fay looked as if something was bothering her, but then it passed. Together we walked across the parking lot, climbed a few concrete steps, and opened a heavy metal door. Inside was a shiny beige hallway with cinderblock walls painted a dark orange.

Aunt Fay walked right to a room marked *Main Office*. "Please tell Florence that Fay Jordan is here," she said to the secretary.

Minutes later a tall, thin woman with wire-rimmed glasses emerged, a big smile on her face. She and my aunt hugged, and then Aunt Fay turned to me.

"Ben, I'd like you to meet Ms. Spencer."

"Nice to meet you," Ms. Spencer said, shaking my hand. I was surprised at how strong her grip was. "I understand your grades have been very good at Lincoln," Ms. Spencer continued. "It's no surprise if you've been living with your aunt for the last couple of years."

"She keeps on me, Ms. Spencer," I admitted. It was true. For years, Aunt Fay was telling me to study and to read.

"Well, you'll be without your study coach from now on. But I'm sure you can do it on your own, Ben." Then she turned to Aunt Fay and said something that almost knocked me over. "So when are you leaving, Fay?"

"*Leaving*?" I asked. Ms. Spencer must have made a mistake.

Aunt Fay winced. It was the same pained look I'd seen when we were outside.

"In two weeks," she replied. "That's something Ben and I still need to talk about," she added, looking at me. "Ben, why don't you look around the school while Ms. Spencer and I catch up a bit."

I nodded and left the office, my head spinning at the news. *Where is Aunt Fay going? Was it far? How could she leave now?* The questions kept coming as I wandered down the quiet hall, passing darkened classrooms and rows of empty lockers.

I moved down the main corridor in a daze when I spotted an open door. Just then, someone rushed into the hallway. I was so surprised, I stumbled backward into a row of lockers.

"I'm so sorry!" said a pretty girl with long braids, her arms loaded with stacks of green file folders. She was wearing jeans and a yellow T-shirt with the words *Bluford Buccaneers* in blue writing on it.

"S'awright," I said, a little embarrassed. "You didn't know I was out here," I added, trying to sound relaxed.

"Yeah, but I need to slow down. There's usually nobody here in the summer, so I'm used to having the hallway to myself," she said, looking at me closely. I hoped she wasn't staring at my bruised face. "Are you a new office aide too?" she asked.

"Office aide?" I almost laughed. "No, I'm a transfer student. I'm about to start my sophomore year here."

"*For real?*" the girl answered excitedly, shifting the stack of folders to her other arm. "That means we're both in the same class, or at least we *will* be in a few weeks. My name's Cindy. Cindy Gibson."

"I'm Ben McKee. I'm glad you're in my class 'cause you're the only person I know in this whole school," I admitted. Cindy smiled, and for a second, Bluford's hallways suddenly seemed nicer. I wanted to keep talking to her, but I wasn't sure what to say. "So . . . what's Bluford like? Do you like it here?"

"It's okay. You got all kindsa people here, you know. Just like any school, I guess," Cindy confessed, pausing as if she was trying to decide what to tell me.

"Last year, I was kinda hangin' with the wrong crowd," she admitted, lowering her voice. "I missed a lot of days and had to go to summer school. When I finished, the principal, Ms. Spencer, gave me a job as an office aide. I think she was tryin' to keep me out of trouble. But she doesn't have to worry. That's all ancient history—"

"Ben? Are you there?" Aunt Fay called out, her voice cutting Cindy off.

Cindy and I glanced toward the sound just as Aunt Fay appeared at the far end of the hallway. Dressed in her suit, she looked strong and important, like *she* was Bluford's principal, not Ms. Spencer.

"That's your *mom*?" Cindy asked. I could hear the respect in her voice.

"No, she's my aunt," I mumbled. "Gotta go."

Cindy smiled, and again the empty hallway lit up. She looked so good standing there that for a second I didn't know what to say. Switching to Bluford didn't seem so bad anymore.

"Well, it was nice meeting you, Ben," Cindy said. "I guess I'll see you around in a couple of weeks, right?"

"Definitely," I replied, turning and following Aunt Fay toward the exit.

"Who was *that*?" my aunt asked as we made our way out to her car.

"Just some girl I met, that's all. Her name's Cindy," I answered.

Aunt Fay smiled at me, and I could feel my face getting warm. She started the car and pulled out of Bluford's parking lot.

"I have a feeling this is gonna be a good place for you, Ben. I just wish I was going to be here to see it," she said, her face suddenly very serious.

In all the excitement about Cindy, I'd almost forgotten what I'd learned in Ms.

Spencer's office. Now it hit me. "Where are you going?" I asked.

"I'm taking a trip back East to see Grandpa for a while. I didn't tell you sooner because you already had your mom's marriage and the move to worry about. I figured that was enough," Aunt Fay explained, putting her hand on my shoulder.

Her touch hurt me inside. Part of me wanted to be angry at her for leaving, and another part wanted to stop her somehow. I barely knew my grandfather. He divorced my grandmother and moved to North Carolina when I was just two years old. When I was really little, he sent birthday cards, but that stopped when I was in second grade. Aunt Fay was the only one who stayed close to him. She told me last year he had Alzheimer's. Since then, she was always on the phone checking on him.

"How long will you be gone?" I asked, barely able to look at her.

"I'm not sure, baby," Aunt Fay replied, and I could see her eyes glimmer for a second. "I don't want to leave you two, but Grandpa's slowly forgetting everything. I want to spend time with him while he still knows who I am," she explained.

I couldn't imagine Aunt Fay being so far away. All my life, she'd been the rock in our family, holding everything together no matter what tried to rip us apart. She saved us after my father walked out. I was just a little kid then, but I can still remember my parents fighting all the time just before he left. Afterward, Mom got depressed and stopped going to work.

"*I don't know what we're gonna do, baby,*" Mom had said. I was only six years old, but I remember being hungry all the time, and the refrigerator was always empty. Then one day the power company shut off our lights. We were living in an apartment without electricity and getting our meals from a food bank when Aunt Fay finally rescued us.

"*Geneva, you and Ben cannot live like this,*" she announced. She'd come over for a surprise visit and found Mom and me sitting in the dark except for a few candles. "*C'mon, you're both coming to stay with Grandma and me. Let's go right now,*" she'd said, picking me up easily in her strong arms.

That was the day we moved in for good, and it was the first time I can remember feeling safe. Now those days were gone—and Aunt Fay would be gone too.

"I'm sorry I have to go, but I know you understand," Aunt Fay said, breaking the sad silence that suddenly filled her car.

"I do," I said, nodding my head.

There were no tears on my face, but inside I was crying.

Chapter 3

"Well, I haven't left yet. There's no reason we can't have a little fun before I go back East," Aunt Fay said.

We had driven in silence for about fifteen minutes. I noticed she was pulling into the crowded parking lot of a shopping mall. Fun was the last thing on my mind.

"C'mon, Ben. You're starting tenth grade, and you're gonna need new clothes, especially with the way you're growing. I figure your mother won't mind if we went school shopping."

School shopping. It was what we did every August. Before Grandma died, she used to come with us too. As soon as the *Back to School* commercials would start on TV, Grandma and Aunt Fay would start getting excited. To them, school was as important as church.

"*God put a good head on your shoulders. It's your job to use it,*" Grandma would say all the time.

"*Grandma's right,*" Aunt Fay always chimed in. "*The reason I'm a teacher is because I got an education and made something of myself. That's what you're gonna do too, Ben.*"

For a while, it seemed that way. When I was little, I was a good student, and they were always proud of me.

"*See how smart Ben is,*" Grandma would say each time I brought my report card home with A's and B's. "*One day he's gonna be president.*"

All that changed in middle school. That's when I started caring more about my friends than my schoolwork. My grades got so bad, I failed sixth grade.

My aunt, Mom, and Grandma were so mad they grounded me the entire summer. No TV, no video games, no computer. Not even a radio. All they gave me were books. For a while, I didn't open them, but then I got so bored I started reading.

I liked it.

My old friends made fun of me. "*Who you tryin' to be?*" they'd say if they caught me carrying a book. But they weren't the ones with Grandma and Aunt Fay nagging them all the time. And they didn't have the guilty feeling I had whenever we went school shopping after my problems in sixth grade. It felt so wrong to see my family spending their money on my new school clothes when all I did there was fail. Maybe it was the books or the guilt, I'm not sure, but I never failed again.

It all happened years ago, but I still remember it like it was yesterday. Aunt Fay did too. I could see it in her eyes.

"C'mon, Ben," she said again. "Let's make sure you're ready for Bluford."

I nodded and stepped out of the car, wondering if it was the last time Aunt Fay and I would shop together.

Hours later, after buying clothes and getting tacos at the food court, Aunt Fay and I drove back to the house. Larry's car was parked at the curb outside when we arrived. Seeing it made my stomach turn.

"Before I go, I want to give you something, Ben," Aunt Fay said as I got ready to leave. She handed me an envelope.

"What's this?" I asked, opening it up.

There was fifty dollars inside. "You already bought me clothes, Aunt Fay. You don't need to be spending more on me," I said, trying to hand it back to her. She brushed my hand aside.

"Keep it, Ben. Call it rainy day money. When you need it, use it," she said. "You're old enough to spend it wisely."

I shook my head but hid the money deep in my pocket. "Thanks," I said, wishing Grandpa would get better and Aunt Fay would never leave.

She smiled at me and then eyed our house. "I think I'll come in for just a minute," she said. "Maybe Larry knows when your Mom's coming home today."

We walked toward the front door. I could hear the TV growing louder as we got closer. I opened the door and found Larry sitting in his chair flipping channels, a beer in one hand, the remote in the other. The TV was so loud my ears hurt, but he didn't seem to care. His eyes narrowed for a second when he saw Aunt Fay.

"Larry, can you turn that down a bit?" she asked. I knew she was checking out the house. There was a barely hidden frown on her face the whole time.

Larry turned down the TV slightly, but it was still pretty loud.

"I hope y'all put some curtains up," Aunt Fay said. The only coverings on the front windows were the tattered green shades that came with the house.

"Yeah, well it's hard to be working and fixing things up at the same time," Larry said. "You're welcome to come in and do it yourself if you want. But I hear you're leaving us soon."

I could tell Larry was happy to say this. You could hear it in his voice. I'm sure Aunt Fay heard it too.

"My plane leaves the Saturday before Labor Day," Aunt Fay said. "I need you to take good care of Ben and Geneva while I'm away."

"They can take care of themselves," Larry replied between sips of his beer. "They don't need you or me doing it for them."

Aunt Fay frowned, but Larry ignored her. He flipped stations a few more times, stopping on a sports channel.

"Tell Geneva I'll call her later," Aunt Fay instructed. Larry grunted and gulped his beer again.

She shook her head and asked me to come out to her car with her.

"I'll try to get back here one more time before I leave," she said when we got outside. "If you need anything before then, call me. Understand?"

I nodded. *We need you to stay*, I wanted to tell her, yet my mouth was suddenly frozen shut. She needed to see her father. I couldn't ask her not to go. But without her, my mom and I were in trouble.

My bruised face and sore legs were proof of that.

An hour later, I was up in my room hiding the money Aunt Fay gave me under my mattress when I heard Larry coming up the steps.

"Do me a favor, Bennyboy. Go up to the corner, make a right, and go about six blocks until you see Cat's sandwich shop. Get some cheesesteaks and a bag of chips for your mom and me. Here's money. Get something for yourself and bring back the change," he ordered, handing me fifteen dollars. It was the nicest he'd ever treated me, so I listened without even thinking about it.

I wish I didn't.

Finding Cat's was easy. Union Street was busy with apartments and a few small businesses, including a laundromat, a check-cashing store, and an old barber shop. But once I turned up the corner, things changed. Except for a liquor store, there were almost no businesses. Most of the houses had bars on their first floor windows.

By the time I'd crossed the six blocks to Cat's, I'd passed groups of kids my age sitting on corners watching me pass. I'd been in the city all my life and knew how to carry myself, but I was a stranger in this new neighborhood. A target.

Walking back in the hot August afternoon with a bag full of sandwiches, I knew I had to move quick. I'd gone about four blocks when I heard someone yell out to me.

"Yo, homie. Whatcha runnin' for?"

I turned to see two guys rushing toward me from across the street. The one who was talking was tall and muscular. He looked like a boxer wearing baggy jeans and a muscle shirt. The other was my height, but with a mean, angry face. He had on jeans, a saggy blue T-shirt, and a backwards hat.

I walked faster, but they kept up with me.

"Boy, I'm talking to *you*," the big kid

yelled out again. He crossed the street and stepped in my path. I was only a block and a half from Union Street. I could see it in the distance, but it was still too far away.

"Man, I don't have time for this. I gotta be somewhere," I said, trying to step around him. I shifted the sandwich bag so my right hand was free, just in case I had to hit someone.

"You ain't goin' nowhere until we say so," the kid said, blocking me and turning to his friend. "Shamar, check out what he's got," he said, nodding toward the bag in my arm.

Shamar tried to yank the sandwiches from my arm, but I held on.

"Get outta my face!" I said, shoving him back.

That's when a fist crashed like a brick against my sore jaw. The hit spun my head around and sent pain shooting through my face. I was still on my feet when someone kicked my leg right where Larry had the day before. It felt like someone was stabbing me, it hurt so bad. I screamed and went down on the sidewalk, dropping the sandwiches.

"Dude is soft," someone said then. They had no idea I was already hurt.

Hands started rifling through my pockets as I struggled to get up. "Get off me!" I yelled, managing to elbow Shamar. He backed away.

"Hit him again, Rodney," he urged. I braced myself.

A second punch exploded into my stomach, and I went down again, fighting for breath. By the time I picked myself up, Shamar and Rodney were gone. So were the sandwiches and all Larry's change.

My heart was pounding when I got home. I was afraid to tell Larry what happened. As soon as I walked in, I spotted Mom sitting on the couch, a Marlboro in her mouth. She looked exhausted as usual.

"What took you so long?" Larry barked as soon as he saw me. He noticed right away I wasn't carrying anything. I wished I could just disappear and never see him again. He came closer. "*Where's our food and my change?!*"

"I got jumped," I explained, embarrassed to say the words.

"*What?!*"

"A couple guys stepped up to me on my way home. I tried to fight them, but they took everything," I admitted. Larry stared at me as if I disgusted him.

"You can't do *nothin'* right, can you?" he yelled, and then he started cursing. "Next time you lose my money, *I'm* gonna kick your butt worse than any of them kids. You hear me, *Bennyboy*?"

My face burned, and I wanted to scream, but Larry's angry stare kept me quiet.

"Oh, Larry. It's not his fault," Mom said, taking a puff of her cigarette. Part of me wanted her to stand up more for me, but I knew she couldn't. What if she said something that set him off again? There was no way we could handle him.

Larry shook his head at me and grabbed his wallet. "I can't stand to look at you anymore," he grumbled. "I'm gonna go get the sandwiches myself. If I find those kids, they're in trouble."

As soon as he left, Mom put her cigarette down and grabbed some ice and a washcloth for my swollen face. "Just don't let him get to you. He'll be all right once he gets some food in his belly," she said.

I couldn't stand to have her babying me, and I didn't want to hear her take his side again. It was all too much, hurting me more than any punches. I got up and headed toward the steps.

Mom shook her head, grabbed her cigarette and plopped back on the couch. She seemed so tired, not just on the outside, but on the inside too. Like it had seeped into her bones somehow.

I climbed the long, hot stairway to my room wondering how Mom and I would survive the sudden changes storming through our lives.

Chapter 4

I stared at the ceiling of my bedroom as the hot sun slowly set outside. Just after dark, a few cars pulled up in front of our house. I heard people laughing downstairs. Larry was one of them. So was Donald.

I hadn't eaten dinner, and I was hungry, but Larry's words from yesterday came back to me.

"There are gonna be days when we're not gonna want a kid around."

I knew it was one of those days. If I went down there looking for food, I'd have to run into him and his friends. They'd see my bruised face. Maybe Larry would tell them what happened and insult me like he did before. He'd make a joke of it for his friends, or maybe he'd do worse.

No way, I told myself. *I'll eat later.*

Instead I turned on the rusty old fan to drown out the noise, and I flipped through the stack of comic books I'd brought from Aunt Fay's apartment. I had started reading comics the summer I failed school. It was the one thing I was allowed to have besides books.

"*As long as you're reading something, you're not letting your mind get soft in front of that TV,*" Grandma would say.

One of my favorites when I was a kid was *Street Knight*. He guarded neighborhoods at night, taking out thugs and bullies with his bare hands. Maybe it was the heat or that I was starving, but the next thing I knew, I started picturing myself facing Shamar and Rodney again. Only this time I had Street Knight's power.

I saw myself stepping out of the alley behind Cat's as they were sitting down with my cheesesteaks. But now I'd be taller. Bigger. Stronger. And no bruises from Larry would slow me down.

"That's not yours," I'd say, surprising them.

Rodney would look around nervously. Shamar might wet himself, his jeans suddenly getting darker.

"Ah, that's nasty," Rodney would say, but he'd be shaking too.

"You fools had any sense, you'd give me back what's mine, right now," I'd warn.

They'd look at each other in disbelief. "Give it to him!" Shamar would whimper.

"Man, I ain't givin' him nothin'," Rodney would shoot back, trying to act hard.

"That's what I hoped you'd say," I'd reply, stepping right up to him.

Rodney's forehead would be covered in sweat. He'd blink, trying to figure out what I might do next. Maybe he'd look around the alley to make sure I was alone.

Then he'd explode, throwing a sucker punch to my jaw like he did before, but I'd be quicker this time.

I'd dodge his right and catch his left in my hand. Then I'd start crushing his fist, making his knuckles snap and pop. He'd cry out. I'd stare at him for a few seconds, letting the lesson sink in.

"Next time, don't take what's not yours," I'd say, letting go. "Now give me my sandwiches and my change."

Shamar would run away, but Rodney would pull out a knife and come at me *again. I'd take his wrist and bend it back until the knife popped out. Then I'd shove him into a pile of trash cans behind Cat's.*

I'd walk up to him then. He'd be cornered, covered in rotten garbage.

"I'm sorry," he'd blurt out then, his hands shaking in fear. "Here. Take it," he'd say, giving me my sandwiches, which were still hot, and my change.

"You sure are sorry," I'd say, without even looking at him again.

The neighborhood would be safe after that. Maybe Larry would hear the news and leave before I came for him.

Whoosh!

An ambulance screamed by on Union Street right outside my window, shattering my thoughts and filling my room with angry red lights.

It was 11:00 at night. I was still hungry. Larry was still downstairs, and Shamar and Rodney were still out there somewhere.

The world *wasn't* safe. That was the truth, and there was no escaping it.

I woke up the next morning with my empty stomach growling. The rest of the house was quiet, and I made sure Larry's car was gone. I figured he and

Mom were at work and it was safe to go downstairs, so I headed straight to the kitchen. The sink was full of dirty dishes, and the air still smelled of cigarettes from the night before.

When I looked for something to eat, I discovered that most of the food Aunt Fay got us was gone. There was still cereal, but someone had finished the milk and the orange juice. I grabbed the last slices of cheese, but there was no bread to eat it on. My aunt's kitchen had never been this empty.

After a bowl of dry cereal and two slices of cheese, I was still hungry. No one would be home for hours, and there was no way I'd ask Larry for food. Then I remembered the money Aunt Fay had given me.

"*When you need it, use it,*" she had said.

I needed to eat.

Ten minutes later I was out the door looking for a place to get groceries. I was carrying twenty dollars and made sure I stayed on Union Street. I asked an old woman at a bus stop where the nearest food store was. She grabbed her purse like I was about to mug her.

"Go to Graham's. It's three blocks

down," she mumbled, barely looking at me.

I thanked her and followed her directions. Graham's was right where she said it was. It had an old-fashioned sign and looked like it had been on the block forever.

A heavy-set woman about Aunt Fay's age was leaving as I walked in. She carried a gallon of milk she'd bought. "You stay safe now, Graham. Tell Alice not to work too hard with them lawyers," she said.

The silver-haired man behind the counter waved to her. As soon as he spotted me, he crossed his arms and watched me through his thick glasses. His eyes focused right on my bruised face. I knew what he was thinking.

No, I'm not going to steal anything, I wanted to tell him.

I picked up a big jar of peanut butter, carried it to the counter, and put it in front of him. "Can I just put the stuff that I want to buy here?" I asked.

"That'll be fine," he said, studying me. "I don't believe I've ever seen you here before. I'm Mr. Graham. What's your name, boy?"

"Ben," I said, grabbing a loaf of bread

and a jar of jelly. "I just moved here a few days ago." He watched as I went back and picked up a large box of cereal and a carton of powdered milk. I piled everything on the counter and pulled out Aunt Fay's money.

"Where you livin', Ben?" he asked as he rang up my food.

"Three blocks up on Union," I said.

He nodded and looked up from the register. His face was lined with wrinkles, but his eyes were bright and clear. "So you goin' to Bluford then?"

"Yeah. Startin' my sophomore year there next week," I said, handing him the twenty-dollar bill.

"Well you'll be in a good school. That's for sure, Ben. I got some old friends over there. Some have been my customers since before you were born," he said with a chuckle, putting my stuff in a paper bag and handing me my change. "Lord knows, I've seen a lot of kids come and go through there."

I pocketed the money, grabbed my bag, and headed toward the door when I heard Mr. Graham grunt behind me. I turned back to see him lifting a carton of bleach and carrying it to a nearby shelf. He looked like he was in pain as he ripped open the carton and pulled out the heavy bottles. Five more cartons were still waiting to be moved.

"You want me to move those for you?" I asked. "They look pretty heavy."

He sighed and straightened his back slowly. I could see the pain on his face. "That'd be real nice of you, Ben. I do feel it in my back more than I used to," he admitted.

I put my grocery bag down and moved the cartons for him.

"I appreciate the help, Ben. A lot of kids your age wouldn't bother helping an old man," he said as I finished. It felt good to hear his words. He even gave me a free grape soda just before I left.

I was carrying my food home wondering how long Aunt Fay's money would last when an idea hit me. I turned around and went straight back to Graham's.

He smiled as soon as he saw me come in. "Back already, Ben? You forget something?"

I didn't know how to say what was on my mind, so I just spit it out. "Mr. Graham, could you use some help around here?"

He gave me a long, thoughtful look.

"Now I appreciate your help earlier, Ben. But we just met. I don't even know you."

I couldn't tell him that I was scared about not having enough food at home. All I could do was keep trying.

"But I'm a good worker, Mr. Graham. I can help you move those big cartons."

"I don't know, Ben," he said, pausing. "I don't like those bruises on your face. I can't have a boy here who's always getting in fights."

"I wasn't looking for a fight," I said. "I took a walk on the wrong block yesterday, and some kids jumped me. It wasn't my fault."

Mr. Graham paused and stared me in the eyes for several seconds. I'm not sure what he was looking for, but I noticed his face soften slightly. "You remind me of myself when I was your age. I was always looking for work. And to tell you the truth, I could use a little help in the afternoon during the school year. But I can't pay you much."

"That's okay," I blurted. "I just need some spending money for . . . school." I didn't want him knowing the truth. That didn't feel right.

"Tell you what, Ben. You come back after your first day at Bluford. Show up around 3:00. There'll be a delivery truck coming in then. We'll see how things go and take it from there."

"I'll be here," I said. "Thanks, Mr. Graham."

Union Street was filled with people as I headed back home. It was mid-afternoon. The air outside was so hot my T-shirt stuck to my back, and I could feel the heat of the concrete through the bottom of my shoes.

Two blocks from my house, someone had opened a fire hydrant, and a jet of water sprayed out onto the sidewalk and poured down the street. Kids of all ages were laughing and splashing in the water. Up ahead, a group of teenagers sat on the shaded steps of someone's front porch, watching me as I approached. I held my bag of groceries close, remembering Rodney and Shamar.

"Wassup, man? Where you from?" said one of the kids. He wore a black baseball cap turned backward. His friends all looked at me.

"'Sup," I said, eyeing them. "I'm right up the block on Union."

"What happened to your face, yo?" said another kid, the oldest one on the porch. "You look messed up."

"That's rude, Roylin," said a girl sitting with them. I knew Roylin was showing off for the crowd. Some kids are like that, acting harder than they really are.

"Yeah, leave him alone, Roylin. He ain't bothering you," said the kid with the cap.

"What's your problem, Dez? I'm just playin' with him, that's all. Besides, what I said's true. He's messed-up lookin'," Roylin said.

"Don't worry about *my* face. You got enough trouble with your own," I said even though I was asking for trouble. Roylin suddenly looked like someone slapped him.

"Aww, snap! That was cold," said the girl. "He just busted on you, Roylin!"

The summer air seemed to get hotter as Roylin stood up and stepped toward me. He was about my size. But before he got in my face, Dez stepped in his way.

"Sit down, Roylin. He wasn't botherin' you until you started with him."

"Dez, I don't care *who* your brother is. Get outta my face unless you want some a what's comin' to him."

Dez looked at me and then at Roylin. He wasn't sure what to do, but I could tell he was on my side. For a second everything was quiet.

Just then a pickup truck stopped in the street next to us. "Wassup y'all?" a voice called out. Roylin's eyes widened, and he walked away without a word. Whoever was driving the truck commanded respect. All the tension in the air seemed to disappear just like that.

"Wassup, Coop!" someone shouted.

I turned and noticed the driver of the pickup looked a lot like Dez, only older and bigger. He glared toward Roylin and nodded at me like he knew exactly what just happened. "Everything all right? You new around here, ain't you? I'm Cooper, but call me Coop. This here's Dez, my brother."

"Yeah, we met," I said looking at them both. "I'm Ben. I just moved in."

"Welcome to the 'hood, Ben," Cooper said, slapping hands with me and turning to his brother. "Dez, we gotta go *now*. I told Tarah we'd pick her up a half hour ago. You know how she gets when I'm late."

"You're busted, Coop," Dez teased and jumped into the pickup with his brother.

"Thanks, Dez," I said as he closed the

passenger door.

"Ain't no big thing," he replied as the truck pulled away in a cloud of gray smoke.

But to me it *was* a big thing. For once, someone was on *my* side, and no fists were flying. *It was the biggest thing*, I wanted to say as I moved through the heat to my house.

Chapter 5

The Saturday before Labor Day came up all too quickly. What I'd been dreading was finally here—the day Aunt Fay would leave for North Carolina. She came to visit us for lunch just before flying out that night.

"I gotta help Donald fix his truck," Larry announced as soon as he learned Aunt Fay was on her way over. I knew he didn't want to be around her, not even to say goodbye.

Mom didn't seem to mind, or if she did, she kept it to herself. By 10:00, she'd gone to the grocery store, cleaned up the kitchen, and started making chicken salad and fresh lemonade, Aunt Fay's favorites. Mom even got a little dressed up. She wore a summer dress instead of jeans and nice shoes instead of her old flip-flops.

If you didn't know better, you'd think we lived in a perfect house. But it wasn't real. At one point, I noticed Mom limping.

"You okay?" I asked.

"Yeah, I'm fine," she said with a forced smile. "I just twisted something at work the other day, that's all. Don't tell Aunt Fay. It's hard enough for her to leave as it is. Let's not give her something else to worry about."

I knew Mom was trying to be strong, but it didn't seem right to lie about something like that. I was about to say something when I heard a knock at the front door. It was Aunt Fay. She was standing outside in a nice white shirt and dark gray pants.

"There he is!" she exclaimed as soon as I opened the door. She gave me a warm hug. "It's so good to see you, Ben."

"You too," I said, swallowing back the sadness building in my chest.

We headed to the kitchen where Mom had set places for the three of us, just like back in the day when we all lived together. Aunt Fay inspected the table settings and looked around the room as if she was searching for something.

"Where's Larry?" she asked.

"He had to help his friend," Mom replied. "He said he's sorry he couldn't be here though."

Yeah, right, I wanted to scream.

Anyone who knew Larry would know Mom was lying. He never said he was sorry about anything. Aunt Fay knew it too. She scowled and shook her head. Mom avoided looking into her face.

"I really wanted to speak to him today," she said, a touch of anger in her voice. "I'm leaving family behind here, and I want him to know that he better treat y'all right."

"He will," Mom said quickly.

Aunt Fay grabbed a notebook from her purse and tore out a sheet of paper. She then jotted down a short letter, folded it, and wrote "LARRY" on the front. "Give this to him," she said to Mom.

I only saw part of what she wrote, words she underlined three times.

Take care of them.

After lunch, while Mom was cleaning up, Aunt Fay pulled a small present out of her purse. "This is for you, Ben," she said.

Aunt Fay was the only one who ever gave me presents. I opened it right up and found a paperback book with a long title, *Narrative of the Life of Frederick Douglass.*

"Ms. Spencer told me this is one of the books you'll be reading in English this fall. I figured you could get a head start by reading it now," she explained.

I looked at the picture of the strong-jawed, bushy-haired black man on the cover. "Who's he? He looks serious," I said.

"He was born a slave and he made himself a free man," Aunt Fay said. "He got power by educating himself, which is what you need to do."

Some things didn't change. Even though she was leaving, Aunt Fay was acting the same as always. "I'll read it," I told her.

She beamed at me then. "I know you will, Ben. I've watched you grow into a strong young man. I know you'll help take care of things around here while I'm gone."

"I will," I said, but my voice cracked.

She gave me a hug as Mom returned from the kitchen. Then she hugged Mom, who had tears in her eyes.

"I've got to be on my way," Aunt Fay said to her. "Don't let Larry act high and mighty, you hear? And call me if you need me."

Mom nodded, wiping her eyes.

But I knew as I watched Aunt Fay's car pull away that Mom wouldn't ask for help. She never did, not even when we were living in an apartment without food or electricity.

With Aunt Fay gone, we were on our own again—on our own with Larry.

The next day, Larry decided to have a party. He said it was for Labor Day, but I think he might have been celebrating that Aunt Fay was gone.

It started around 3:00 in the afternoon when Larry came in with a couple cases of beer. It wasn't long before some guys I'd never seen before pulled up and started drinking with him in the living room, their voices growing louder as the day wore on. Around dinnertime, Donald came over with pizzas and more cases of beer.

"Whatcha lookin' at, Bennyboy?" Larry said to me when I passed through the kitchen where he and Donald were playing cards with a few other guys. Money was sitting in the middle of the table, and no one was talking. I thought

I saw Donald hiding some cards, but I didn't say anything.

"Nothin'," I said. His voice was louder than usual. I knew the beer was getting to him.

"That's what I thought. Now, don't you have somewhere else to go?" he asked, pointing toward the stairs. I knew not to argue.

It wasn't until Monday that the house was empty. When I finally came downstairs, I found pizza boxes, beer cans, and dirty ashtrays all over the living room. The air stank of stale alcohol and cigarette smoke. But worse than the smell was a tense feeling in the house, like the air before a bad storm.

That's when I first heard the yelling. It was coming from the hallway upstairs.

"Larry, you got things all wrong. I was just talking to him, that's all!" It was my mom's voice, and she sounded scared.

"Next time, you don't even *look* at him. You hear me?" Larry ordered. His voice was ugly and rough, still slowed by the beer he'd drunk the night before. But there was something else in it. Something dangerous. "*You hear me?!*" he repeated.

"Larry, please just relax. I would never—"

Whap!

The sickening sound could only be one thing. He was slapping her.

"Stop, Larry! Don't do this!" Mom screamed.

Whap!

I felt like I was going to throw up, but I rushed toward the stairs just as Mom came rushing down with Larry right behind her. As she reached the bottom of the steps, I stepped in between them to shield her.

"*Leave her alone!*" I yelled, my voice so loud my ears hurt.

Larry turned on me like a pit bull. With my arms out to keep him from Mom, my face was unprotected. His punch landed just below my right eye, snapping my head back so hard my neck hurt.

"This ain't none of your business, *Bennyboy!*" he cried.

"When you hit her, it *is* my business," I said.

Larry sent two more lightning-quick punches to my stomach, and I fell to my knees. I could barely breathe.

"Please, Larry. He's just a boy. He

53

didn't mean it," Mom pleaded.

For a second, time seemed to stop, and I wondered what Larry would do next. Then I heard knocking at the door. Larry almost looked scared at the sound.

"Yo, Larry, you in there?" a voice called from the front porch. It was Donald.

Mom rushed for the door. She probably hoped he'd help us somehow. A second later Donald was standing in our messy living room. His coal-black eyes darted back and forth as he tried to figure out what was happening.

"I don't mean to be buttin' in or nothin'," he said, looking around at us. "Lar, I just thought we'd head out. Maybe hit the track or something."

Somehow, Donald's words broke the spell, and Larry's anger seemed to fade.

"Yeah, let's get out of here," he said. Then he glared at me and Mom. "When I get back, I wanna see this place straightened up."

As soon as they left, I raced over to Mom.

"You okay?" I asked, looking at her face. She had a bloody lip. "We need to call the police or something, Mom. If you don't, I will," I said.

"You don't understand, Ben. He's not usually this way. It's just the beer. He had too much to drink. He's totally different when he's not drinking," she said.

"But Mom, look at your face! Look at mine!" I said, grabbing the phone. "I'm calling them right now."

"No, Ben! We call the police, it'll only make things worse around here," she said, taking the phone from my hands. "Besides, I'm all right. All he did is slap me a little. He just got a little jealous because he thought I was talking to one of the guys he invited over last night. He gets so jealous . . ." she said, wiping her eyes.

"Mom, he shouldn't treat us that way. It's not right," I said.

She gently touched my face. I could feel one eye swelling. "Oh, Ben. You're just like Aunt Fay. But things aren't always as simple as she says. I wish things could be better for you here."

She turned away from me then and started cleaning up the dirty house. I was too upset to speak, but I helped her. Together, without a word, we swept up and cleaned the downstairs and filled three large garbage bags with the trash from the weekend.

Afterward, Mom took a shower and set herself up in the living room chair with the TV and her cigarettes. I headed upstairs to my room with some ice cubes in a plastic bag for the swelling on my face.

I stayed in my room for the rest of the day. But my head was full of questions that kept racing by like the cars on Union Street.

What were we going to do about Larry?

How could I keep Mom safe?

How can we survive like this?

I didn't have any answers.

Chapter 6

The next morning, Tuesday, I woke up at 5:17 in the morning, and I couldn't get back to sleep. It was my first day at Bluford High, and I was nervous. For once, I didn't even want to eat anything.

When I looked in the bathroom mirror before getting in the shower, I noticed my cheek was still a bit swollen, and there was a bruise beneath my right eye. But it didn't look as bad as the day before. I hoped no one would notice.

After my shower, I put on a new pair of jeans and a baggy black T-shirt I bought with Aunt Fay. I followed a group of six other sleepy kids down Union Street and made the turn to Bluford. As I neared the school, I spotted Ms. Spencer at the front doors next to the metal detectors, helping direct traffic.

Two security guards and a few teachers were with her.

"Good morning, Ben," she said as I passed by, and then she turned to speak to other students she knew.

I walked down the main hallway I'd visited weeks earlier, trying to act like I knew where I was going. Although I wasn't the only new student, it sure felt that way. Everyone seemed to have someone else to talk to—everyone except me.

The schedule I had gotten in the mail said my first class was English in room 214 with a teacher named Mitchell. It seemed simple, but when I looked at the signs in the hallway, they made no sense. One said "C Wing," another said "A Wing." Neither said where room 214 was. I started to sweat. I didn't want to start out Bluford being the only sophomore who couldn't find his first class. I was about to ask a janitor for help when I heard someone call me.

"Ben?"

I spun around to see Cindy, the office aide I'd met the day Aunt Fay and I visited the school. She was standing with another girl, and both of them were smiling at me.

"Wassup, Cindy!" I said, grateful to

see someone I knew, especially her. "How you doin'?"

"I'm fine, I guess. But I wish I didn't have to get up at 6:30," she said with a tired grin. "After the summer, I'm not used to that."

"I hear what you're sayin'. I'm so tired, if I closed my eyes right now, I'd pass out," I said, trying to keep her smiling. I turned my head slightly, hoping she wouldn't notice my swollen cheek. If she did, she hid it well.

"My whole freshman year was like that," said Cindy's friend, a girl I'd never seen before. "I don't know why school can't start at, like, 11:00. I could get used to that."

"Oh, I'm sorry. Ben, this is Jamee. She's my girl. We go *way* back," Cindy explained.

"All the way to middle school," Jamee added. "Nice to meet you."

"You too," I said, glad to know someone else. I wanted to talk, but I knew our first class was about to start, and I had no idea where it was. "Look, maybe y'all can help me. I'm supposed to be in Mitchell's English class in room 214, but the signs around here don't make sense. Do you know where it is?"

Jamee tilted her head and blinked at Cindy. "Tell us where it is, *Ms. office aide?*"

"Hmm, let me think," Cindy said playfully. "That would be the class we're in next period. You're in *our* English class!"

"You're lucky, too. Mr. Mitchell's cool. You coulda got Mr. Osgood. Then you'd be even more sleepy first period," Jamee said. "C'mon. Follow us."

The halls were full of students as we walked to class. At one point, we were crammed together, and my shoulder gently bumped Cindy's. I apologized, and she flashed me the same smile that lit up the hallways over the summer. I couldn't help but notice the curves of her body in her jeans and tank top. She looked good.

"Here we are," Jamee announced, as we turned into a classroom. I noticed a tall black man with an orange necktie standing in front of the chalkboard. The room was already half full with kids as Jamee slid into a chair. Cindy sat next to her, and I grabbed the next closest seat, two rows behind her. The bell rang a few minutes later.

"Good morning, ladies and gentlemen. I'm Mr. Mitchell," he said, closing the door and writing his name on the board. "Welcome back!"

Several students in the class moaned, as if school was the last place they wanted to be.

"Now it's okay to not want to be here today," he said in a confident voice as he looked around the room. "But it's *not* okay if you don't make the best of it." He then began going around the room and shaking hands with each student, asking us to give our name first. My palm was a little sweaty, so I rubbed it on my jeans before he got to me.

"Ben McKee," I said to him, as he clasped my hand. He smiled at me, as he did to everyone. I saw him notice the bruise under my eye.

"Welcome to Bluford, Ben. Lincoln's a good school, but I like to think we're even better," he said.

I was surprised he knew where I'd come from. Then I remembered how Aunt Fay talked to Ms. Spencer and got that book for me. They must have talked about my classes. It was like she was still watching out for me, even from North Carolina!

Mr. Mitchell began class by going over what he expected. Show up on time. Hand in homework on time. Lots of class participation. Lots of reading and writing. The usual stuff teachers say.

"We must read to exercise our brains," he added at one point. It was like listening to Grandma again. Some kids rolled their eyes. But then he turned and asked us a strange question.

"What's the most dangerous creature you can think of?"

The class was silent. We all looked at each other. What was he talking about? What did this have to do with English? What did it have to do with anything?

"I'm serious," he added. There was a long pause before someone finally spoke up.

"Sharks," said Reggie, a kid in the back of the room. I'd heard his name when Mr. Mitchell shook his hand. "I heard some kid got his foot bit off in Florida just last week."

"Boy, what do you know about sharks?" someone shot back, with a chuckle.

"Snakes," said another kid. "I seen this one on TV that spits poison in your face, and one bite can kill like five hundred people."

"You're trippin'!" said a kid next to

him.

"I hate snakes," Jamee said. "Yuck."

The class started talking then, even though it had nothing to do with English. After a few minutes, people were getting silly, trying to pick the scariest animal. Someone even said something about an alien from a movie, when Mr. Mitchell cut in.

"No, keep it real," he said. "Is there anything scarier?"

One thing came to mind for me. *Larry.* He was the scariest animal I knew, but I wasn't going to tell anyone about him.

"How about people?" I said.

The class got quiet again and everyone looked at me. I could feel eyes scanning me, the new kid.

"*People?*" Mr. Mitchell asked, nodding. "You think they're the most dangerous, Ben?"

"Definitely," I replied. "You don't see animals blowing up buildings or fighting wars. If you ask me, people are the scariest thing out there."

"But he said *animals.* People ain't animals," said Reggie. He sounded annoyed.

"*Some* of them are," Cindy cut in. "At least some of the ones I know."

A few kids laughed, and then Mr. Mitchell jumped in.

"Reggie, Cindy, and Ben make interesting points which I want to discuss further." He passed out copies of something called "The Most Dangerous Game." "But read this short story first. It will make you wonder whether there is a difference between people and animals, and who is more dangerous."

We then read a few pages of the story, and Mr. Mitchell asked us to write down our predictions about what might happen next. We also had to list any proof we had for our ideas.

The part we read was about a hunter who sails near this island that everyone says is evil. Then in the middle of the night, he hears gunshots in the dark, and he falls off his boat into the sea. The water is described as "blood warm," so I wrote what I guessed would happen next: the hunter would end up on the island and face the shooter. I also wrote that someone was going to die. The blood made me think that. Just as I finished writing, the bell rang. My first class at Bluford was over.

"Good job today, Ben," Mr. Mitchell said as he glanced at my paper. Reggie scowled.

I managed to find my next classes—biology, geometry, and history—without any help. I even answered a question in Mr. Najar's history class. He was talking about different cultures and asked us if anyone knew where Mesopotamia was.

Most kids couldn't even pronounce it, but I knew because Aunt Fay taught me. It's one of the first places people settled, and it's in Iraq where everyone is fighting. Aunt Fay taught me even older settlements were in Africa—that all the world's people came from there originally. I started to say this when I noticed kids looking at me. At Lincoln, my friends were used to me speaking up about things I knew, but at Bluford I was too new for that. All I got were stares, so I shut up.

By lunchtime, I was starving, but I had no one to sit with. I joined the crowd and moved slowly through the line. All around me kids were finding the friends they hadn't seen since last year. It felt like I was the only person who had no one to talk to.

Lunch was a gloppy-looking beef stew on top of soggy noodles. I took my tray and looked for an empty table when

I saw a face I recognized. It was Dez, the kid who stood up for me on the street the other week. He had some change in his hand, and he was heading to a nearby snack machine. He spotted me the same second I saw him.

"What's happenin'?" he asked with a nod. He started to walk away but then stopped, glancing at the bruise under my eye. "You all right?"

"I'm cool," I said, wishing I could hide it from everyone. "Just trying to get settled in. New school and all, you know."

"Let me give you some advice," he said with a smile. "Skip that stew."

"Yeah, it looks kinda nasty," I agreed, laughing.

I looked at the crowded cafeteria then, searching for an empty table. The nearest one was against a wall in a back corner. I started walking toward it when I heard Dez's voice again.

"You sittin' with someone?" he asked. I turned around.

"Just this stew."

"Sit with us, then."

I didn't argue. By the end of the lunch period, I met Tyray, Darrell, and Harold. I even learned that Jamee and Dez were kind of going out, that Tyray and Darrell used to hate each other, and that Harold once liked Cindy.

"I'm over that," he said when I asked him about it.

"You hurt yourself?" asked Tyray, a quiet, muscular kid, just before we left the cafeteria.

"Yeah, I took an elbow playin' a little one-on-one with my stepdad," I explained. The other guys gave me a funny look for a second, but no one mentioned it again.

Several hours later, the final bell rang, and I joined hundreds of kids who rushed out Bluford's main doors. My first day of school was over, and it wasn't that bad. With Cindy and a crew to eat with in the cafeteria, I almost forgot about home and what waited for me there.

As I walked back, I was glad I'd talked to Mr. Graham and that he'd asked me to meet him after my first day at Bluford. It meant I had somewhere else to go besides home with Larry and his beer.

I got to the store a little after 3:00. Mr. Graham spotted me right away.

"Hello, Ben," he said, with a happy and surprised look on his face. "I wasn't sure I'd see you again, but here you are.

C'mon, there's a truck pulling up right now."

We walked outside to a boxy truck full of soda cases.

"All that's gotta come in, and I'm afraid your back's stronger than mine. A couple years ago, I could do this in my sleep. Things are a little different now," he said, shaking his head.

"I got it," I said, jumping into the back of the truck.

I tried to impress him by grabbing as many heavy cases as I could and rushing them into the store, but I nearly crashed into an elderly woman buying a bag of cat food.

"You don't have to hurry, Ben," he assured me as soon as she left. "Like I told my daughter Alice this morning, people today rush everything. Things would work out better if everyone slowed down a little, you know—just move along quietly."

Two hours later, my arms and back were tired, but I'd finished unloading the truck, stocking the shelves, and sweeping the floor—everything he asked. He shook my hand and said he'd like to hire me for three days each week.

"I'll give you five dollars an hour if

you want the job. It's all we can afford, Ben," he said.

It was fine with me. Thirty dollars a week would give me enough money for food. I left the store and headed home in the steamy late-afternoon heat with his words still echoing in my head.

"*Just move along quietly.*" It made sense.

But then I got home.

Larry and mom were watching TV when I walked in. They both looked tense.

"Where you been, Ben?" Mom asked.

I told her about my day at Bluford and my part-time job at Graham's. She seemed both happy and sad at the same time. A couple times, she smiled, but then wiped her eyes like she was crying. When I told her how well things went at school, she gave me this look that still haunts me.

"*Save yourself, Ben,*" it seemed to say. "*I'm not gonna make it, but as long as you survive, it's okay.*"

Larry didn't budge the whole time I talked. Instead, he just flipped channels.

"I'm proud of you," Mom said, wiping her eyes again with a tissue.

I knew something happened, but I

69

was afraid to ask with Larry sitting there, his face stormy.

"It's good you got your own money," he barked. "That's one less thing *we* have to pay for." Then he held up his index finger and pointed to the steps. It was a signal for me to get out of his part of the house.

I wanted to scream. Since we moved, I hadn't seen him spend a cent on me, so he had no right to talk or tell me where to go, but what could I do?

I bit my tongue and dragged myself to my room. Mom came up an hour later.

"I'm sorry, Ben. Here, you must be starvin'," she said as she came in. She was holding a plate with a chicken sandwich made from leftovers. I took it and put it on the floor. I'd already eaten two peanut butter and jelly sandwiches I made myself, but I didn't tell her.

"Mom, what's wrong? I thought y'all would be happy I'm working."

"I *am* happy," she admitted. "But it's Larry. He got real bad news today."

"Huh?"

"He got laid off from his job this afternoon," she said. I could see her eyes glisten, but then she took a deep breath and looked at me. "He's upset, but he says they'll call him back soon," she added, trying to sound hopeful.

"How you know he got laid off? Maybe he got fired," I said bitterly.

"*Ben.*"

"I'm serious, Mom. Maybe he showed up drunk on the job. I see him drinking in the middle of the day sometimes," I told her. My anger was coming out. "Maybe he came to work stinkin' like beer, or maybe he tried to boss someone around like he does here—"

"*Ben!*" she said, raising her sad voice at me. It hurt me inside to hear it. "It's hard enough around here without you making it worse. Now, we've got to make the best of things until he gets back to work."

I was quiet then, holding back my own angry tears.

"Things are going to get pretty tight," she added, rubbing her shoulder as if it was sore. "I'm going to have to pay the rent and bills with my salary."

"I got money—"

"No, Ben. Your money's for you," she said quickly. "But if you can just . . . take care of yourself with what Mr. Graham is giving you, that would really help."

Four words caught me. *Take care of yourself.* It was like she was admitting I was on my own, that she couldn't care for me. I know it hurt her to say this to me. Her eyes were puffy and glassy with tears waiting to fall.

"I can manage, Mom," I said.

She put her hand on my shoulder. It almost burned where she touched me.

"You make me proud, you know that?" she said.

I shrugged, grabbing the book Aunt Fay gave me, anything to avoid looking into Mom's defeated eyes.

Chapter 7

Larry didn't go back to work the next week—or the week after.

Instead, he was home all the time.

I was glad for the three days I worked after school because I barely saw Larry. And Mr. Graham gave me free snacks, unlike home, where there was even less food than before. But the days I didn't work at the store were different.

Sometimes Larry would ignore me when I came in. Other days he'd talk to me, just to have somebody listening while he complained. And some days, especially when he'd been drinking, he'd lose it and beat me.

Fridays were always the worst. That was the day Mom got her paycheck. He'd pick her up after work, and they'd go to the grocery store together to do the shopping. Mom did her best to get food, but they also came home with cartons of cigarettes and twelve-packs of beer. Larry always took a chunk of cash from her paycheck for himself.

Mad money, he called it.

One Friday night, there wasn't enough money for what he wanted. I heard them arguing downstairs, and Mom stepped out for a few minutes. That's when he raced up the steps to my room. I was eating a sandwich I made when he stormed in.

"What's this?" he said, looking at the open peanut butter jar still sitting on my drawer. "You got your own private kitchen up here this whole time?"

There was an ugly look on his face. He put his hand on my chest and shoved me backward so I went sprawling on my mattress.

"You don't want me comin' downstairs, so I started keeping some stuff up here," I tried to explain.

"Money's tight right now, so don't you be holdin' out on us," Larry sneered. He put his heavy shoe on my chest and pressed down until I started gasping for air. "From now on, any food you get goes in the kitchen for *all* of us. I'ma check your room from now on too. If I find food up here again, you'll be sorry."

"But you're the one who told me to stay upstairs," I said.

He pressed down harder, and I felt a burning in my chest. "Don't you dis me, boy! I ain't playin' with you anymore," he growled. "How much old man Graham pay you today?"

None of your business! I wanted to say. But I felt like my ribs were about to snap. "Thirty dollars," I gasped. It was the entire week's pay.

"Give it here," he ordered, a strange look in his eyes. I wanted to curse him out, but I was too scared. I handed over the money, and he drew back his foot.

I heard someone come in the door downstairs. A second later my mom called out, "Larry, Ben, you guys up there?"

Larry shoved my money in his pocket.

"You're living under this roof. You help us out now and then," he said before he headed back downstairs. I shut my door behind him, my heart pounding in my sore chest.

Later that night, I heard noise and laughter coming from downstairs. When I crept down to the second floor to use the bathroom, I found out why. There was a smell of beer in the air. Larry had used my money to get drunk. I wanted to throw up.

At 3:00 a.m., I woke up to the sounds of slaps and cries coming from downstairs. At first I thought it was a nightmare, but then I realized it was real. Larry was beating up Mom.

I stumbled in the dark to my doorway and heard another dull thud followed by a whimper.

"Mom, are you okay? Is everything okay down there?" I yelled.

The whole house suddenly got quiet. I stepped to the edge of the staircase when she called out.

"Stay out of this, Ben. Everything's gonna be fine." I could hear she was crying. In the darkness, my mind was filled with horrible images of her huddled in a corner bleeding. I started to go down the steps when Larry's voice thundered up at me.

"You heard your mother. Get your butt back in that room. *Now!*"

"Please, Ben, go away. Just go back to your room," Mom begged.

I sat on the top step, unsure what to do. When Mom cried out, I cried too, and when Larry hit her, I put my hands over my head to block out the sounds. I wanted to call out her name, but no sound came from my mouth. Finally, I heard Larry go back down to the first floor and turn on the TV. And from the second floor, I heard the awful sound of my mom weeping.

"Stay away, Ben," she whimpered when I tried to come to her. "Just stay away."

Hours passed.

At some point I heard a roar outside and went to my window. Two police helicopters were hovering just above the row homes across the street. Maybe they were searching for Larry. Maybe Mom finally called the police.

"He's here!" I wanted to tell them.

As I watched, something went wrong. The helicopters got too close. Their rotors hit, and they crashed into each other and fell right onto the houses in a bright orange fireball. A river of fire spilled out in all directions, rushing across the street toward my house. I knew I had to get Mom before it was too late.

I reached the second floor, but the fire was too fast. It boiled onto the steps and chased me back all the way up to the third floor. I closed my door and felt the surging flames smack against it. Then the door began to melt and give way, and Larry was there, fire coming out of his hands, ready to burn me to ashes.

There was nowhere to run. Flames climbed the walls and windows. I was trapped and felt the pain as my skin began to blister and melt.

"NO!!!"

I screamed and woke up, shivering and drenched in sweat. The house was quiet. I was still at the top of the steps where I'd fallen asleep. I rubbed my eyes and walked back to my room. I knew what the dream was telling me. A fire was destroying my world, and I had to stop it.

But how?

I left my house around noon on Saturday. I couldn't stand to be there, especially with Mom pretending her fat lip and swollen cheeks were normal and Larry sleeping off his hangover on the couch.

I didn't know where to go, so I just went to Graham's.

"There he is!" Mr. Graham said with a smile when he saw me. "You okay,

Ben? You look a little tired."

"Yeah, just didn't sleep too well last night," I said.

He looked at me with his bright eyes for a bit longer than usual.

"What is it, Ben? You never come here on a day off. Something on your mind, boy?"

I wished a customer would come in and distract him. I couldn't tell him what happened last night. But I didn't want him to send me home either. The store was one place I could go where people talked nicely to each other, a place where no one punched or screamed, a place I was wanted.

"I was just thinking maybe I could work some more, you know. You don't have to pay me or nothin'," I said.

He studied me again, and I prayed he wouldn't ask any more questions.

"I can always use your help, Ben," he said with a warm smile.

I don't know why his words made me want to cry, but they did. I fought it off though, and for the rest of the day, I worked harder than ever. I got a blister on my hand and tore the sole of my shoe against the edge of the door, but it didn't matter. It felt good to lift boxes, stock shelves, and clean up messes.

At the end of the day Mr. Graham thanked me. "You're the hardest working young man I know. Nothin' wrong with honest work, is there Ben?" he asked. "Say, what are you doing for supper? Why don't you come over tonight? Alice is cooking up a storm, and I know she wants to meet you."

Mr. Graham had mentioned his daughter Alice before. I'd never met her, but I'd seen her in old pictures he kept near the cash register. He even showed me a fancy card once with her name on it. It said she was a paralegal, whatever that is. I felt a little funny about going to his house, but I didn't want to go home, and I was hungry.

"Call your folks and let them know you're comin' over," Mr. Graham suggested. I nodded but didn't make the call. I knew they'd hardly notice unless I was late, and I was afraid Larry would answer the phone.

We locked up the store and walked a few blocks to Mr. Graham's house. It was on a quiet street lined with small one-story houses. His yard was the nicest one, full of pink and white flowers. As he opened the door, I smelled roasted chicken, and my stomach started growling.

"Alice, we're here!" he called out. A woman about Mom's age stepped out of the kitchen, wiping her flour-covered hands on a dish towel. I recognized her face from the pictures in the store.

"Hello, Dad. How was your day?" she said warmly, looking over at me.

"Great, thanks to Ben here. He helped me all day. I wanted you to meet him, so I thought we'd have him over for dinner.

"*It's about time!* Lord knows I made enough food," she replied. "Nice to finally meet you, Ben," she said, shaking my hand.

"You too," I answered nervously. "Thanks for having me over."

"Ben, I'm going upstairs to get changed," said Mr. Graham. "I'll be down in a few minutes."

Alice chuckled. "It's the same thing every day. First thing he does when he gets home is change out of his work clothes. He's been doing it as long as I can remember," she said. "Well, while he's doing that, let's finish up in the kitchen. If you want, you can help me mash the potatoes."

"Okay," I said following her down a short hallway lined with family pictures.

We stepped into a kitchen as clean and bright as Aunt Fay's. A small wooden plaque hung over the sink. *God Bless This House*, it read. On the stove, I spotted the source of the great smell: a golden-brown chicken fresh out of the oven. My mouth started watering. I swallowed hard and tried not to stare, but Alice saw my expression.

"I hope you're hungry, Ben," she said with a smile, lifting a big pot off the stove.

I was. Since Aunt Fay left, I'd been slowly losing weight. I was never fat, but my jeans already felt looser than when we first bought them. School lunches and my food stash didn't make up for the missed meals and empty cabinets at home. And now Larry had taken everything.

"I've drained the potatoes, Ben," Alice said, breaking my thoughts. She was standing in front of a big bowl filled with steaming potatoes. "You think you can mash 'em up for me?"

"No problem," I replied. She handed me a masher, and I got started.

"Dad's always talking about how

helpful you are," she said as I crushed the potatoes against the side of the bowl.

"To be honest, I'm glad you're around," she continued. "It makes me nervous with him alone in the store all the time. I asked him to hire someone after Mom died, but he's stubborn. He likes to pretend he's forty-five, not seventy-five.

"Other than our family, you're the first person he's ever let work in there. That store's his baby. He put me and my brother through school by workin' there seven days a week. Know what he said the other day? He told me you work as hard as him. Now that's sayin' something, 'cause he's worked like a dog all his life."

"I like working with your dad. It's like he's a grandfather or something, not a boss," I admitted. "And it's nice having money too."

"I heard *that!*" she said with a little laugh. She added some milk and butter to the potatoes and asked me to mix them again. As I did, she pulled out a tray of fresh biscuits from the stove and took it into the dining room. A minute later, she grabbed a steamy bowl of buttery corn. My stomach felt like a big empty suitcase that needed to be filled.

"Ben," she said, adding a little salt and pepper to the potatoes. "You might not want to talk about this, but Dad's a little worried about you."

I knew where she was going, but I kept my eyes down on the potatoes.

"Worried?"

"He says he sees bruises on you a lot. We know you're not a troublemaker," she said, pausing as if looking for the right words. "Honey, who's been hitting you?"

Her question rang in my head. Part of me wanted to tell her the truth, but where would I start? And what could *she* do anyway? My jaw locked shut, and the heavy silence stretched out longer and longer as I kept mashing. Finally she rested her hand on my shoulder.

"Never mind, Ben. If you ever want to talk about it, you know where we are. Dad or I will be glad to listen."

"Thanks, Miss Alice," I mumbled, my face burning.

She took a spoon and tasted the potatoes.

"Perfect!" she announced. "C'mon, Ben, let's eat."

It was the best thing she could have said.

Dinner was as delicious as I'd

expected. Sitting at the table with Mr. Graham and Alice, talking and laughing about the store, mopping up gravy with one biscuit after another, I felt happier than I had in months. But I knew it couldn't last.

As the evening wore on, I started thinking about my mom and Larry at home not far away. By the time I left around 8:00, I was depressed.

Larry and my mom barely looked up from the TV when I came in, the house stinking of cigarette smoke.

"Wondered where you were, Ben," Mom mumbled, half asleep, between puffs. Larry didn't look for a moment in my direction as I headed upstairs.

For once, my stomach was full, but I knew that would change now that Larry took my food. And if he kept taking my money, I'd be in real trouble. The one good thing was that I still had thirty dollars from the money Aunt Fay left me. With that, I could buy food on the way home from school if I had to.

I lifted my mattress to check the money when I discovered it was gone. Some of my drawers were open too, like someone had just gone through them. I knew what happened.

Larry robbed me!

"No!" I said out loud, but no one heard me.

My pulse pounded in my head, and I kicked my pillows and punched my mattress in frustration.

"That's not right!" I yelled out.

The loud TV below drowned out my voice. If it didn't, Larry would have come up and given me another beating. I knew it, but I almost didn't care anymore.

My room was a prison cell, and it felt like it was getting smaller.

Chapter 8

On Monday I woke up hungrier than ever. My money and food were gone, and I'd missed dinner Sunday night because Larry was in one of those moods where anything set him off.

"I'm sick of people sayin' they ain't hirin'," he had complained after being skipped for a job as a security guard somewhere. He smelled of beer, and I bet the person he spoke to noticed, though Larry wouldn't admit it.

I got so hungry that night, I decided to do something I'd never done before: get free breakfast at school. Back at Lincoln, I knew kids who showed up at school early for a free meal. Bluford had the same program. I'd seen the forms the school sent home at the end of the summer and thrown them out. Food was never a problem—until now.

Before Mom even got out of bed, I showered, threw on my clothes, and headed out the door to Bluford. The shoe I'd damaged at Graham's on Saturday started coming apart, but I didn't have time to worry about it. My mind was on eating.

I rushed to school and was about to enter the cafeteria when a group of girls rounded the corner and nearly ran into me. They were all dressed in sweats. Some wore *Bluford Cheerleading* T-shirts. Cindy and Jamee were with them. Cindy spotted me first.

"Ben!" she called out, surprised. All the girls stared. Cindy had that friendly smile on her face. "I can't believe you're up this early too. Jamee dragged me here for cheerleading practice. What about you? You here for football practice?"

My stomach dropped. I shook my head slowly. I didn't know what to say.

Jamee understood before Cindy. I saw her look toward the cafeteria and then at my face. She knew I'd come to eat.

"Cindy, come *on*," Jamee urged, tugging her by her shirt. "We've gotta get back to the gym."

"Wait!" Cindy said to her. "What's wrong, Ben?" she asked.

My words stuck in my throat. I gave an awkward shrug and glanced in the direction of the cafeteria.

"I . . . couldn't sleep so I . . ."

"C'mon Cindy. *Now*," Jamee said. The other girls turned away.

Cindy looked confused for a second. Then I saw her get it. Her jaw dropped. Her eyes opened wide. The smile melted away.

"*Ohhh*," she said, stepping back. "Uh . . . I . . . gotta go, Ben." Her face changed then. She stopped looking at me. "See you later," she said and then hurried off.

I felt like a zombie as I walked into the cafeteria and got my tray of scrambled eggs. As hungry as I was, I suddenly lost my appetite.

The rest of the day, people seemed to avoid me. It felt like the whole school was looking down at me, though no one said anything to my face except Reggie.

I was on my way to Mr. Mitchell's class when my ripped shoe started making a slapping sound each time I stepped. Reggie followed me to class and heard it.

"Wassup, Slappy," he called out. "Gonna suck up to Mitchell again, Slappy?"

Reggie pointed my shoe out to other kids. I ignored him and took my seat, but he kept laughing as class started.

At one point, Mr. Mitchell asked me to come to his desk for a second. He was handing back a quiz I scored a seventy-eight on, my lowest grade in years. He wasn't happy, but I pretended not to notice. All I wanted was for my shoe to keep quiet, but Reggie wouldn't let it go.

He clapped his hands lightly each time my sole slapped the floor. Other kids started laughing, and I noticed Cindy wouldn't even look at me. I wanted to kill him.

"We can do without the sound effects, Reggie," Mr. Mitchell said.

Reggie stopped, but the rest of the class was onto the joke. A couple guys started slapping their hands against their jeans to make the sound. Other kids started giggling.

In the hallway after class, Reggie kept at it. "You gonna slap your way to history now, Slappy? Maybe kiss up to your teacher in there too, huh, *Slappy?*"

I stopped in the hallway, my blood boiling, my hands shaking.

"What's the matter, Slappy? Yo Mama can't afford no shoes and no breakfast?"

"*Ouch!*" someone shouted at his comment, which hit me like one of Larry's punches.

I turned around. People started moving back, giving us space.

"Aww, yeah! Here we go!" someone cheered.

"Whatcha gonna do, *Slappy?*" he said. He didn't think I'd do anything, I could tell. His hands were at his side. I stepped forward, grabbing him by the throat, and shoved him back into a locker with a loud crash.

"You say one more thing, I'll *slap* the teeth outta your mouth."

Kids cheered at my words.

"*Fight!*" they yelled.

"Hold up!" shouted a familiar voice. I felt arms yanking me back by the shoulder. I turned to see Dez and Darrell.

"Man, he's just a punk, Ben. Don't let *him* get to you."

A second later, a teacher and two security guards pushed through the crowd. Kids scattered in all directions, trying to stay out of trouble. But Reggie and I were caught.

"You two. In the office. *Now!*" the teacher yelled.

Five minutes later Reggie and I were in front of Ms. Spencer.

"What's the problem?" she asked.

"Just a little misunderstanding," I said.

"Yeah, that's all it was," Reggie chimed in. "No big thing."

We both pretended to know nothing.

"Well, since this is the first time I'm seeing you both, let's make this clear. You fight, you're out. That's the kind of ship I run here. Reggie, you should know that. Ben, you better learn real quick. I'll let this go, but don't wind up here again. Understand?"

We both nodded, and she sent us back to class. As we walked down the hallway, I heard my shoe slapping again. This time, Reggie kept quiet, but it didn't matter. The damage was done.

To Cindy and the rest of the school, I was Slappy. The kid whose mom was poor, the one with bruises on his face. The one who needed free breakfast.

I wanted to escape from everything, but there was no way out.

When I got home from school, Larry's

car was gone. Inside, I found Mom stretched out on the couch half asleep. I was exhausted too.

"Hi, Ben. How was school?" she asked, fighting back a yawn. It was a question she hardly asked any more.

"*Fine*," I said, taking off my ripped shoe and walking toward the kitchen. She picked up her cigarettes and followed me.

"How come you're home so early?" I asked as I grabbed a pair of scissors.

"I didn't feel good this morning, so I called out sick," she explained as she sank into her kitchen seat.

I knew she was still recovering from the beating Larry'd given her. Through the cloud of cigarette smoke, I noticed a purple smudge under her left eye. She'd tried to cover it with makeup, but I knew it was a new bruise. I was sure there were others I couldn't see. Larry wasn't stupid. He never left too many marks where people could see them. The middle of the body, the chest, back, and legs—those were his favorite targets.

I cut the loose rubber off the sole of my sneaker and looked at her.

"Mom, why don't we just leave?" The words just popped out of my mouth.

She shook her head as if my words annoyed her.

"*Please*, Ben," she said wearily rubbing her forehead like she had a headache. "That's just crazy talk."

"*Crazy?* I'll tell you what's crazy," I snapped. "Crazy is staying here with a man that hits you and hits me and lies around drinking while you work. *That's* crazy."

"That's enough, Ben!" she said angrily. "Don't talk that way about Larry. He's a good man. He's just going through a rough patch now. Things'll get better when they call him back to work. You'll see."

"A good man doesn't slap his woman around!" I shot back. "He doesn't steal money neither!"

"It's not all his fault, Ben!" Mom said, her voice cracking. "It's hard on a man's pride to be out of work. And then he gets to drinking to try to make himself feel better, and he just loses control sometimes. Honestly, he feels as bad about it as you do."

"Don't give me that!" I yelled, slamming the scissors down on the table. "What's it gonna take before you stop making excuses for him? Huh? You want him to knock my teeth out? Maybe split my head open—"

"Stop it!" Mom yelled. "*Just stop it!*"

Tears were streaming from her eyes. Her head was in her hands, and she sobbed like a child, her chest heaving.

I suddenly hated myself.

"I'm sorry, Mom," I said. "I didn't mean to yell. I just . . . want you to be okay."

She cried for a while. I stood next to her, feeling like my head would explode.

"It'll get better, Ben. I know it will," she said desperately. "I know Larry's a good man. You'll see. Just give me some time. I'll make this marriage work."

I didn't believe her, not for a second.

In school the next day, I couldn't focus on anything. Mr. Mitchell was saying something about Frederick Douglass, but my head echoed with the sound of my mom crying. At lunch, I didn't say a word to anybody, not even Dez, who kept trying to get me to talk.

"You all right, Ben? Whatcha thinkin' about, bro?" he asked a few times. I shrugged him off.

After school, I got to Graham's at the usual time. Mr. Graham gave me that worried look too, but I didn't feel like talking so I stayed in the back stocking cans of tomato sauce. I didn't notice time passing until it was almost 6:00. I'd worked an extra hour. That's when I heard the familiar bell ring and the front door open.

Then I heard something strange. A gasp, followed by Mr. Graham's voice, more tense than usual.

"There's nothing much here," he said.

I stepped forward to see a big man wearing a black ski mask over his face. He was standing at the counter waving an open switchblade at Mr. Graham.

"Shut up, old man, and open up that cash register," the guy said. "*You* stay right there, boy," he added, pointing the knife at me.

I stood still, afraid to move.

"Son, you don't have to do this. There's a better way," said Mr. Graham, staring at the man with a mixture of sadness and disbelief.

"*Fool*, I didn't give you permission to talk. Hand over the money! *Now!*"

"Just give him the money, Mr. Graham," I called out.

Mr. Graham took a slow, deep breath

and opened the register. But the stocky man was in a hurry. When he saw the cash, he shoved Mr. Graham aside, grabbed the bills, and ran. As he dashed out the door, I caught a brief glimpse of his dark eyes. For a split second, I almost thought I recognized them from somewhere.

"Ben . . ." Mr. Graham called from behind the counter, his voice scratchy and weak. He hadn't gotten up.

I rushed to his side and could tell something was wrong. He was clutching his chest, and his eyes stared crazily at the ceiling.

"Mr. Graham? Are you okay? *Mr. Graham!*" He didn't answer.

I grabbed the phone from under the counter and dialed 911. In minutes, an ambulance and two police cars pulled up.

"He's in here!" I shouted out to them. Mr. Graham didn't look good. His eyes were half opened, and his skin had turned slightly gray, but he was still breathing.

"You're gonna be okay," I kept saying to him, hoping it was true.

A crowd gathered outside to see what was happening. People groaned as Mr.

Graham was carried out to the ambulance. The police had a lot of questions for me, and I told them everything I knew. Then I called Alice.

"Oh my Lord, is he okay, Ben?" she asked when I told her what happened.

"I don't know," I said to her. "I don't know."

I was up in my room later that evening when I heard a car pull up outside. A moment later Larry was calling up to me, in a strange voice.

"Ben, come down here. You got some people here to see you," he said.

A small group of strangers were standing on our front step. Larry stood in front of them at the door, his arms nervously crossed on his chest. My mom was next to him. They both looked a little embarrassed. I could tell they were trying to hide the people's view of the beer cans on the table.

I only recognized one face in the crowd—Alice. She smiled warmly at me.

"Hello, Ben. I just came back from the hospital. I wanted to tell you my father's okay. He had a mild heart attack, but the doctors say he's going to be all right. They said if he didn't get help quick, it would have been much worse, so thank you for being there," she said, giving me a hug. "You got a good boy here," she said, turning to Larry.

He gave her a fake smile.

"I know I do," Mom replied. Her smile was real.

"Anyway, the first person Dad asked about when he woke up was you, Ben," Alice continued. "He's in room 424 at City General Hospital. Maybe you can visit him."

"I'd like that," I said to her, looking at all the strange faces staring at me.

"Oh, I'm sorry, Ben. Some of our friends wanted to meet you after I told them what happened," she said. She introduced them quickly, and I shook their hands. They all lived within a few blocks.

One man told me he was Dez's uncle, a police officer from another district.

"Ben," he said, "can you tell us any more about what happened? We're real upset about this. Mr. Graham is like everyone's grandfather. His store's one of the last places left in this neighborhood where folks can still get real food around here. It's a shame this happened to him, of all people."

Everyone nodded as he spoke. They shared his anger.

"I wish I saw more, but the guy's face was covered. All I know is he was big and had these dark eyes," I said, hiding one detail—the feeling that I'd seen them before. I still wasn't sure. "I'll be looking for those eyes everywhere. Believe me."

"When we get this guy, he's in big trouble," Ms. Alice cut in. "This was more than a robbery. When he pulled that knife and touched my dad, it became a felony. Once we catch him, he's going away for a long time."

Larry listened carefully to everything. As soon as everyone left, he started complaining.

"Can't you keep this place looking any nicer?"

I headed upstairs, but I could still hear his voice.

"Sometimes I'm embarrassed to be living with you."

I turned the fan on to drown out the sound, but he was still yelling.

"Why's everyone making such a big deal about an old man anyway?"

I shut my door.

Chapter 9

My hungry stomach woke me up early the next morning. The sky was just beginning to glow when I sat up in my bed, my head still spinning with what happened at the store.

Who robbed Mr. Graham? Those familiar eyes still haunted me.

After a quick shower, I raced out of my house to get breakfast at Bluford. This time, I got there earlier and used a different hallway to get to the cafeteria, anything to avoid Cindy. After the awkward way she left me in the hall, I didn't want to see her. I couldn't handle her and her friends looking down at me. It hurt too much.

The cafeteria at Bluford was half full when I got there. I moved through the line quickly and grabbed my plate. Breakfast was two spongy pieces of French toast and a greasy slab of sausage. As hungry as I was, it made my mouth water.

I took my tray and headed out to find a seat when I saw Tyray. He was alone at a nearby table with his own plate of French toast. I couldn't believe it.

"Wassup?" I said, feeling a little strange. In the weeks we'd eaten lunch together, he was always the quiet one at our table. "I didn't know you came here."

"I didn't know you did either," he replied and then gulped down some orange juice. "Guess we all got our secrets, huh?" he added mysteriously.

"What do you mean?"

He looked at me for a few seconds as if he was sizing me up.

"You still playin' half-court with that stepdad of yours?" he asked.

I knew what he meant.

"That's none of your business," I snapped back.

"I'm just bein' real, bro. Everybody knows what you're goin' through. It don't take no genius to see it," Tyray said. It was the most I'd ever heard him say. "I know lotsa people try to get in your face and find out your business. Most of them don't know what they talkin' 'bout. But Mr. Mitchell does. If you really gotta talk to someone, talk to him. Trust me, I know."

"Why you tellin' me this?" I asked.

"My dad used to play half-court with me," he said, swallowing the last of his food and getting up. He left the cafeteria without a word.

I was speechless.

In English, Mr. Mitchell gave us a pop quiz on the first section of *Narrative of the Life of Frederick Douglass*. I hadn't even started reading the book.

For the first time since sixth grade, I was way behind in school, especially in Mr. Mitchell's class. No one knew why I couldn't focus on school, and I couldn't tell them the truth. That would make things worse for Mom and me.

Instead, I tried my best on the quiz, but I felt my stomach sinking when I handed it in with four blank answers out of ten. When class ended, Mr. Mitchell asked to speak to me.

"What's going on, Ben?" he asked. My quiz was on top of his desk with a score of fifty. "We both know you can do better than this."

"Sorry, Mr. Mitchell," I said, hoping

he would just let it go. "I forgot to read that section."

Mr. Mitchell studied me closely. He wasn't happy with my answer, but his eyes weren't angry. They were worried.

"You seem to be forgetting a lot these days, Ben," he said, flipping through his grade book. "Your grades keep slipping, and you seem really distracted lately. I'm concerned about you, and I'm not alone. Is everything okay . . . at home?"

I had to push back the sudden tears I felt in my eyes. I prayed he didn't see them.

"Everything's cool. Just a bad quiz, that's all. No big deal," I replied quickly, escaping toward the door.

Mr. Mitchell shook his head. I could tell he didn't believe me.

"I'll do better on my next one. You'll see," I said. Just then a group of students from his next class entered the classroom. I was grateful to see them.

"I gotta go," I said, rushing into the hallway.

After my last class, I stopped at my locker to drop off my books when I heard someone call my name. I turned to see Cindy. She looked nervous.

"Ben, are you okay?" she asked. "I just heard about what happened at Graham's last night. That's so scary."

"You sure you wanna be talkin' to me? What if *your friends* see you? I got *free breakfast*, remember?" I said the words extra loud, shutting my locker with a loud crash.

"Ben, I didn't mean to—"

"To what?" I challenged. "You didn't mean to make me feel like trash in front of all the cheerleaders? Is that it?"

"Ben, I'm so sorry—"

"Look, Cindy. I don't need your apology, and I don't need you feelin' sorry for me. Unless you got somethin' else to say, there's nothin' for us to talk about."

Cindy looked hurt. I almost felt bad for her, but I couldn't stop. There was just too much pain inside, even though most of it wasn't even her fault.

She started to walk away, but then she stopped herself and came back to me.

"What are you doing Saturday?" she asked.

"*Huh?*"

"Jamee's having a little party at her house, and I want to go there with you. That's why I came here," she said, nearly knocking me over.

"Girl, don't play with me. I'm not your charity case," I said, ready to leave her there in the hallway.

"*No!* It's not like that!" she yelled. "I was about to ask you three days ago, but I just got too nervous. Then the whole thing happened yesterday in the hallway, and I didn't know what to do. I freaked out because I was afraid I'd ruined everything. That's not what I want."

I didn't know whether to believe her. She was close to me, and I could smell her sweet perfume and see she meant what she said. Part of me wanted to tell her why I was really upset, but I couldn't. It was all too much, too close.

"Girl, I'm sorry. I gotta go. Let's talk about this later," I said.

Cindy's eyes glimmered for a split second as if there were tears in them. "Listen, Ben. I can understand if you're mad, but don't think I was lookin' down at you," she said. "If you knew about my life, you'd understand I have no room to look down on anyone."

"I'll catch up with you later," I replied, heading outside. I had to get away.

There was only one person I could stand to see.

I made the twenty-block walk to City General Hospital. When I found room 424, Mr. Graham was lying in bed wearing a blue hospital gown. He had tubes hooked to his arm, and a small screen at his side showed how fast his heart was beating. He looked smaller than I remembered, and older, too. Seeing him, I felt a sad knot in my chest.

"Hey, Mr. Graham," I said. "How are you feeling?"

"Better today, Ben," he replied with a big smile. His eyes were alert again, but tired. "C'mon in. Sit down for a while." He pointed to a chair at the foot of his bed. "They tell me you handled yourself real well after that fellow left the store."

I didn't feel I did anything special. I wish I could have stopped the whole thing somehow. "I'm just glad you're okay," I admitted.

"Don't you be worrying about me, Ben. It'll take more than this to keep me down," he said, as if his heart attack was no big deal. "Besides, I can see you got your own things to think about right now."

I could feel him looking at me, but I didn't dare look back. Outside, the

107

afternoon sun was beginning to cast long shadows. Mr. Graham broke the silence.

"I remember one day when I was about five or six," he said. "There was this rain comin' down somethin' fierce. All of a sudden, the sun broke through the clouds, and a rainbow appeared. An older boy told me there was a pot of gold at the end of the rainbow. And do you know, I believed him! I went runnin' off barefoot through puddles and across fields trying to reach it. But with each step I took, that rainbow moved further away.

"For years, I lived my life that way, thinking the pot of gold was just around the corner and I'd scoop it up and be on Easy Street. But I was just dreamin'," he continued.

"After I got out of the service and met my wife, rest her soul, I got my head out of the clouds. That's when I stopped being a dreamer and started being a doer. I decided to open a little store that would be of value in the neighborhood. Instead of dreaming about it, I *made* it happen. That's what you need to remember, son. You got to *make things happen.*"

His voice had grown stronger as he

talked. When I finally looked up at him, he was focused on me, kindness in his eyes.

"And you know what else, Ben?" he added, with a friendly smile. "That's what you're gonna do one day. I know it. These old bones don't lie."

Make things happen.

Mr. Graham's words kept echoing in my head as I made the long walk back home. They didn't seem to fit me. I couldn't seem to make anything happen. At home, I was just trying to stay out of the way, and at school, I was barely scraping by. Now, with Mr. Graham in the hospital, I didn't even have a job.

Make things happen.

How? I wanted to say, frustrated at the new voice in my head.

On my way home, I passed by Graham's store. It looked strange with all the lights out and the "Closed" sign hanging inside the door. I stopped for a moment, my mind flashing with memories of what happened the day before.

In my head, I could see the large man with the knife in his hand. I could hear him threatening Mr. Graham again. I could see his eyes glance at me for a split second. Was there fear in them?

It hit me then.

The eyes.

I *had* seen them before. It all made sense.

Make things happen, the voice urged me again. This time I had an idea.

When I walked into the house, I knew I had a dangerous game to play. Larry was in his chair finishing off a beer. His head was tilted way back so he could gulp down the last drops.

"Where's Mom?" I said. It was almost 7:00, and she should have been home for at least an hour.

He belched and then looked at me. "She's upstairs taking a rest," he said.

I knew what that meant. He'd hit her again, probably just minutes ago while I was walking home.

My blood began to boil. It was the same as every day, but this time I didn't run up the steps. I just stared at him.

He glared back with a sneer on his face. I could see his anger building, but so was mine.

"What kind of man are you?" I said. "Beating up on a woman and a kid?"

He jumped out of his chair and

shoved me against the living room wall with a loud thud. Before I could move, he was in my face. I could see the veins in his neck pounding.

"You feelin' brave, *Bennyboy*? It's about time you had a *real* lesson. I been lookin' forward to this for a while now," he growled.

But for once I didn't feel helpless.

"I ain't scared, Larry!" I snapped. "But *you* should be since I might know who robbed Graham's."

Larry froze. I could see his mind racing.

"It was your boy, Donald, wasn't it? I'm guessin' you told him when to show up. Only neither of you knew I was workin' late. I'm thinkin' maybe I should tell the cops," I threatened.

I watched his face carefully for clues. His bloodshot eyes were already filled with anger. But there was something else in them for a split second—a flash of fear.

"Boy, you don't know *nothin'!*" he roared, his face inches from mine, his spit flying in the air, his stinking breath filling my nostrils.

He started hitting me then, his fists slamming into my chest and stomach.

One punch landed deep in my gut, knocking the air right out of my lungs. Another shot crashed into my ribs. I heard a crunching sound and felt a stab of pain shoot into my side. I put my hands over my head, but I couldn't stop the rain of punches.

"You're just blowing smoke, *Benny-boy*. But if you get the law on me with your crazy idea, you and your mom going to be in more trouble than you can dream about. *You hear me?!*"

I couldn't even speak. I just shook my head *yes*.

"That's what I thought," Larry said with a wicked grin. "I got some news for you too. Your mom and I don't like this neighborhood. We're moving this week-end over to the south side. You can forget all about your buddy Graham. Startin' next week, you'll be in another school."

My legs were weak, and I was still gasping for air, but his words hit me hard.

"Now get outta my sight!" he ordered, shoving me toward the steps.

Hours later in my room, I stared at the ceiling, watching the shadows racing by with each car that passed outside.

My side ached whenever I moved, and

all the muscles in my stomach were bruised and sore. But inside I hurt more.

Larry was going to rip Mom and me away from everything again.

My new friends would be gone. Mr. Graham and Alice, my new family, would be gone too.

No more Mr. Mitchell.

No more Bluford.

Just a world of pain, nothing more.

Next to my bed was my copy of the *Narrative of the Life of Frederick Douglass*. I remembered my failed quiz and how I told Mr. Mitchell I'd read the book. Now it didn't matter. Nothing did. I flipped the pages anyway, my eyes catching on a single sentence.

My natural resilience was crushed, my intellect weakened, my desire to read vanished, the cheerful spark in my eye died away.

Tears rolled down my face at the words. They described me.

Chapter 10

The next morning, my ribs were so sore I had trouble getting out of bed. I wanted to get to school early for breakfast, but I couldn't move fast enough. At one point, I sneezed, and it felt like my whole chest was ripping apart. The pain brought tears to my eyes.

Downstairs, I saw Larry hadn't even gone to bed. He was sprawled asleep on the living room couch. The TV was still turned on.

At school, Dez and Tyray spotted me trying to walk down the hall.

"Oh, man, Ben. What happened?" Dez asked. "You okay?"

"Fell down the steps."

Tyray rolled his eyes and looked at Dez. They knew the truth.

"C'mon, Bro. Let's get you to the nurse

114

or somethin'. You gotta tell somebody."

"*No!*" I snapped. It hurt to talk. "Just leave me alone."

In English, I hunched over my desk, trying to hide the pain. The class was discussing Frederick Douglass, but I had nothing to say. Out of the corner of my eye, I saw Mr. Mitchell, Jamee, and Cindy watching me. They looked worried.

In the middle of Mr. Najar's class, Ms. Spencer knocked on the door and came in.

"Ben McKee, come with me," she said firmly. "There's a visitor here to see you."

The class stared and whispered as I slowly got up. We walked down the hallway together. I could feel her watching my every move, so I tried my best to walk normally.

"You okay on your feet, Ben?" she asked. "You look like you're in a lot of pain."

"Yeah, I fell down the steps," I said. "Ain't no big thing."

Ms. Spencer sighed and shook her head. "I wish I'd known about it sooner. There are some times when you boys just need to speak up and trust us adults."

I kept quiet as she led me into her

office. But as she closed the door, I turned and almost fell over at what I saw next.

There in a dark blue business suit was Aunt Fay!

"Oh, Ben!" she said, throwing her arms around me. I closed my eyes and felt tears suddenly streaming down my face. I couldn't stop them if I tried. Nothing could.

"This is my fault, too. I should have known when your mother called me last week. She never calls," Aunt Fay said, her own voice shaking. "All this time you've been a quiet young man of steel. But steel's not enough. You've got to know when to ask for help. This is the time, Ben. Tell us exactly what's been going on."

"It's nothin'. I just . . ." My voice broke up. I couldn't lie anymore. Not with the tears in my eyes. Not with Aunt Fay in my face.

"Ben, pull up your shirt. Let us see what's hurting you so bad," Ms. Spencer said.

I looked at them both. I knew what they would see if I pulled the shirt up. All the swelling and the ugly fist-shaped bruises and welts. For a second I couldn't move.

"Please, Ben. Let us help," Ms.

116

Spencer urged.

"It's okay, Ben," Aunt Fay said, her eyes glistening. "You're safe now."

I closed my eyes and slowly raised my shirt, grunting at the pain.

Ms. Spencer gasped.

"Lord have mercy," Aunt Fay said.

"Mr. Mitchell and his students were right, Fay," Ms. Spencer said. "After I spoke with Ben's other teachers, I knew something bad was happening at home. That's when I called you," she added. "But I didn't realize it was *this* bad."

Fire burned in Aunt Fay's eyes, and she hugged me again, gently this time.

"Is he doin' this to your mother too?" she asked me, her voice full of rage.

I nodded.

Aunt Fay shook her head angrily. "Florence, call the police right now!" she ordered.

Ms. Spencer grabbed the phone and started dialing. The closed office was suddenly quiet, except for the hum of the florescent lights overhead. For a few long seconds we waited as Ms. Spencer's call went through. I knew what I would have to do next. Tell the truth to the police. Make it happen. Just like Mr. Graham said. But I was scared.

"This is the principal at Bluford High School," said Ms. Spencer into the phone, cutting the awkward silence. "I have a case of domestic violence to report. The victims are one of my students and his mother."

She then told the officer what she knew and handed me the phone. "You need to tell the police what's been happening, Ben," she said. "Tell them everything."

I took the phone. My hands were shaking, and my throat was suddenly dry. I didn't even think I could talk.

"Go on, Ben," Aunt Fay urged, gently rubbing my back. "Do this for yourself and your mom."

I raised the phone to my ear.

"Hello?" said a man's voice. "Ben? Are you there? This is Officer Whittington. I want to help you," the voice continued. "Hello, Ben?"

"Go on," Aunt Fay repeated. Ms. Spencer nodded.

I took a deep breath and let the truth spill out.

First I described each beating and each threat. Aunt Fay moaned as I mentioned the night I spent on the steps listening to Larry punch Mom. Then I described the hold-up at Graham's and that I'd seen Donald behind that ski mask. I also revealed what Larry's eyes proved to me—that he'd sent Donald to do his dirty work and rob the store.

Officer Whittington asked lots of questions. I could tell he was writing everything down. When I was done, he said I was brave and that he'd like me to come to the station. He then asked to speak to Ms. Spencer.

"You probably saved Geneva's life," said Aunt Fay as they spoke. "That man is outta control, and from the sounds of things, he's getting worse. I don't even want to think about what woulda happened if y'all moved again," she added with a shudder.

"The police are sending a car to the house right now to pick Larry up," Ms. Spencer announced, hanging up the phone.

After the school nurse did a quick examination of my ribs, Aunt Fay and I left Bluford and went straight to the house to meet Mom. She would be home from work soon, and we wanted to be there the second she stepped off the bus.

"Your mother's world's bein' torn apart again. She's gonna need us more than ever," Aunt Fay explained as we left. "Better she hear everything from us instead of the police."

As we pulled up to our house, I noticed a black-and-white patrol car parked at the curb. Two officers were inside. Larry's Dodge was missing.

"Why are they just sitting there?" I asked, but I knew the answer. Larry hadn't been caught.

Aunt Fay looked tense. She parked her car and told me to stay inside. She then got out as one of the officers rushed over to us. I listened as Aunt Fay introduced herself. I could hear them talking low, and then the officer's radio crackled to life. A voice came through loud and clear.

"Suspect has been apprehended."

The officer asked a few quick questions and nodded and smiled.

"Looks like they just picked him up at a liquor store six blocks from here, Ms. Jordan!" he announced.

"Thank the Lord," Aunt Fay replied with a sigh, wiping her forehead. I felt weeks of stress drain from my body.

"You all can relax. From what Officer Whittington says, Larry Taylor's not gonna be bothering you or Mr. Graham anymore," he added, heading back to his car. Seconds later he drove off.

"Lock him up and lose the key. Any man who beats his wife and kid like that doesn't deserve to be on the street," she fumed as she returned to the car. "There are *no* excuses."

It felt so good to hear her say what I'd known for so long. It was a dream come true.

"Thank you for coming back for us," I said, my voice breaking. "I missed you, especially your cookin'," I added, feeling myself smile for the first time in weeks.

"I missed you too, baby," she replied with a grin of her own. "You know, *that's* a good idea. I haven't had a bite to eat since I left North Carolina early this morning. And I know *you're* hungry. I'll go get us some sandwiches. Then when your mom gets here, we'll eat as a family. Afterward we can go back to my place and figure out what happens next."

"Sounds good to me," I replied, grateful she was in charge again.

"You wait here for your Mom, but don't tell her what happened until I get back," Aunt Fay said. "Let's do that together."

I nodded and got out of the car. For

once, I wasn't afraid. Aunt Fay was back, and Larry was behind bars. We were finally safe.

Even my ribs felt better as I went back inside and went up to my room. I was getting clothes for the night when I heard something that stopped me cold.

A familiar metal thud.

I knew the sound. Larry's Dodge.

How could it be? Did the police make a mistake?

I looked out my bedroom window and spotted Larry dashing toward the front door. He was gazing up at me, a crazed look in his eyes. I was trapped!

My room wasn't safe. The door was half broken already, and Larry knew it. He'd smash through in seconds. I had to move somewhere else. Fast.

I rushed to the second floor, my ribs aching with each step. I heard the front door downstairs slam. He was in the house. Time was running out.

Without a sound, I crept into Larry and Mom's bedroom and hid against the wall. He thundered past on his way to my room.

"*You're done, Ben! I told you not to snitch!*" he yelled like a wild man. "*Cops just busted my best friend 'causa you!*"

I heard him two-step up the stairs to the third floor. In seconds, he'd figure out I wasn't there.

Move! I told myself. I flew out of his bedroom and ran downstairs as fast as my feet would take me. He must have heard the noise.

A second later, he was coming down too. I couldn't outrun him, not with the knives of pain slicing into my ribs.

I landed on the bottom step and dashed across the living room. I was ready to bolt out the front door when I saw Aunt Fay coming up the steps. I couldn't let Larry get to her.

Never.

There was no more running for me. Instead, I turned to face him.

Larry reached the bottom step and darted at me. I threw one punch, hoping to buy Aunt Fay some time. It hit his jaw, but he didn't even blink. He swung his right hand like a sledgehammer at my face. I raised my arm to block it.

Crack!

Pain exploded through my arm as the blow knocked me backward into our TV. I crumpled to the floor, my arm broken and useless.

"Leave him alone!" Aunt Fay yelled.

"You got two minutes till the police throw your butt in jail where you belong. I called them myself when I saw your car."

Larry turned on her with an ugly sneer. "Woman, you got *no* sense. I told you to stay outta my business, but you wouldn't listen. You deserve what's coming to you."

He moved toward her, but Aunt Fay didn't flinch. She stepped directly up to him, her eyes blazing.

"Yeah, go on! Hit a woman, you coward! Hit me and add ten more years to your jail time." She jutted her jaw at him and put her hands on her hips, standing there defiant in her suit.

For a second, Larry hesitated, but I knew it wouldn't last. Aunt Fay was making a mistake. His arms tensed up then. He was about to strike. I had a half second to act.

With his back turned, Larry couldn't see me stand up, gritting my teeth against the pain. He couldn't see me lower my good shoulder. He couldn't see me hurling my body.

But he felt it.

I rammed my shoulder right at his knees, knocking his legs out from under him. He tumbled on me, crushing my chest and arm, but I didn't care anymore.

"Get out of here, Aunt Fay!" I screamed. "*Go!*"

Larry scrambled to his feet, rage in his eyes. His boots were inches from my face. I remembered the day he kicked me on the steps and saw the sick idea spread across his face. I knew what was coming, and there was nothing I could do to stop it.

He's gonna kill me, I thought.

Larry leaned forward ready to stomp. I braced myself and lowered my head when Aunt Fay threw herself over me.

"*Don't touch him!*" she yelled, protecting me with her body. We were cornered.

Suddenly there was movement and shouting at the front door.

"Taylor, freeze right now!" The two police officers from before burst into the room, clubs drawn. "Don't even think about moving," one said to Larry. Within seconds, they cuffed him and led him away.

That's when Mom came rushing up the steps, a look of panic on her face. The second she saw us on the floor, she began sobbing. Her eyes focused on my swelling arm.

"*What did he do?*" she wailed. "*What*

did he do?!"

Aunt Fay grabbed her and held her tight.

"It's over, Geneva," she said. "You and Ben are safe now."

Aunt Fay drove us straight to the emergency room, where my arm was x-rayed. A nurse gave me a shot that took away the pain. Then a doctor set the break in a cast. Mom cried the whole time, but Aunt Fay talked to her and calmed her down. Afterward we sat in the car and ate the sandwiches Aunt Fay bought. It didn't matter that they were soggy. They were the best sandwiches we'd ever tasted.

Later, at the police station, Officer Whittington came up and introduced himself.

"There was a mix-up. The man we picked up at the liquor store was Donald Gates, not Larry Taylor," he explained. "Mr. Gates has given us a full confession. It turns out your stepdad planned the entire robbery. He's been charged with aggravated assault and battery against you and your mom and with felony robbery against Mr. Graham. He'll be going away for a long time. Count on it," the officer promised.

With Aunt Fay's encouragement, Mom signed statements saying that Larry assaulted us. I watched as she nervously scribbled her signature on each page. When we finally walked out of the station, Aunt Fay was between us, holding our hands. It was the three of us again, like the days before Larry. Mom was quiet, but there was a soft look in her eyes. I think she was beginning to remember life without fear.

On Aunt Fay's face was a quiet determination.

"The world's such a dangerous place, you know," she said to us. "That's why we have to stick together. I need to be here for the two of you. We're family, and family sticks together."

Maybe it was the painkiller or maybe it was Aunt Fay's words, but my spirit soared. The pain and fear were finally gone, as if a spring rain had washed them away. I thought of Mr. Graham, Alice, and everyone at Bluford. I had much to tell them and many people to thank, people who cared when I was in trouble, even though I pushed them away.

And I had other things to do too. Like go to that party with Cindy and her

Have you read the other books in the Bluford Series?

(continued on the following pages)

SHATTERED

Paul
Langan

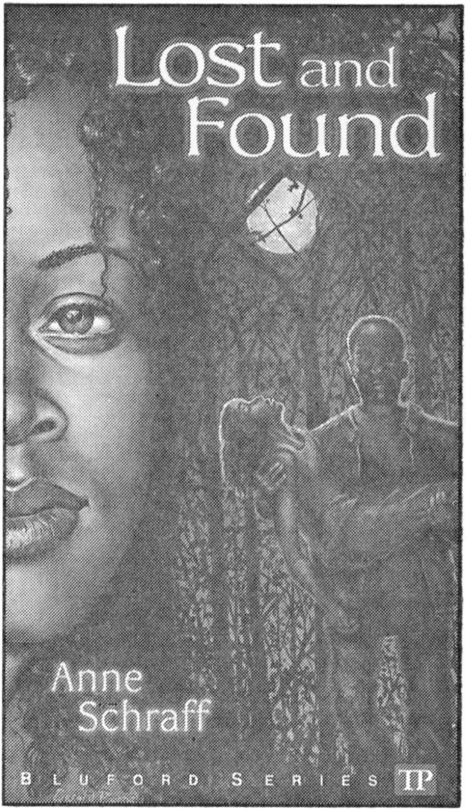
Lost and Found
Anne Schraff
BLUFORD SERIES
TP

A Matter of Trust

Anne Schraff

Anne Schraff

Someone
to Love Me

B L U F O R D   S E R I E S   TP

The Bully

Paul Langan

TP BLUFORD SERIES

The Gun

Paul Langan

Until We Meet Again

Anne Schraff

Paul Langan & D.M. Blackwell

Blood Is Thicker

BLUFORD SERIES TP

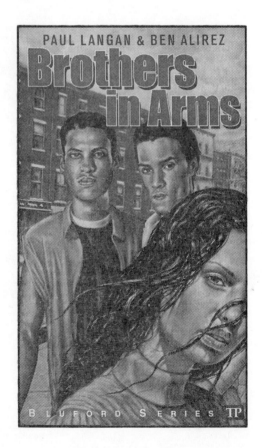

PAUL LANGAN & BEN ALIREZ

Brothers in Arms

PAUL LANGAN

Summer of Secrets

The Bluford Series

Lost and Found
A Matter of Trust
Secrets in the Shadows
Someone to Love Me
The Bully
The Gun
Until We Meet Again

Blood Is Thicker
Brothers in Arms
Summer of Secrets
The Fallen
Shattered
Search for Safety

The Townsend Library

The Adventures of
    Huckleberry Finn
The Adventures of
    Tom Sawyer
The Beasts of Tarzan
Black Beauty
The Call of the Wild
Dracula
Ethan Frome
Everyday Heroes
Facing Addiction:
    Three True Stories
Frankenstein and
    Dr. Jekyll & Mr. Hyde
The Gods of Mars
Great Expectations
Great Stories of Suspense
    & Adventure
Gulliver's Travels
Incidents in the Life of a
    Slave Girl
It Couldn't Happen to Me:
    Three True Stories
    of Teenage Moms
Jane Eyre
The Jungle Book
The Last of the Mohicans
Laughter and Chills:
    Seven Great Stories
Letters My Mother Never Read

The Merry Adventures of
    Robin Hood
Narrative of the Life of
    Frederick Douglass
The Odyssey
The Prince and the Pauper
The Princess of Mars
Reading Changed My Life!
    Three True Stories
The Red Badge of Courage
The Return of the Native
The Return of Tarzan
Silas Marner
Sister Carrie
The Story of Blima:
    A Holocaust Survivor
Surviving Abuse:
    Four True Stories
Swiss Family Robinson
A Tale of Two Cities
Tarzan of the Apes
Ten Real-Life Stories
Treasure Island
Uncle Tom's Cabin
Up from Slavery:
    An Autobiography
The Warlord of Mars
White Fang
The Wind in the Willows
The Wizard of Oz

**For more information,
visit www.townsendpress.com**

Boynton Beach City Library
Books may be kept two weeks and may be renewed up to six times, except if
have been reserved by another patron. (Excluding new books and magazine
A fine is charged for each day a book is not returned according to the above
No book will be issued to any person incurring such a fine until it has been pa
All damages to books beyond reasonable wear and all losses shall be made g
to the satisfaction of the Librarian. Each borrower is held responsible for all it
charged on his card and for all fines on the same.